The Pint-sized Piglet

and Other Animal Tails

GRACE FOX ANDERSON, first editor of
Winner Books, is editor of *Counselor*,
Scripture Press' take-home paper for
children 8 to 11. She has been in church-
related ministries with children for over
25 years. Mrs. Anderson received her de-
gree in Christian Education from Wheaton College, in Wheaton, Ill. Her stories
and articles have been published in a
variety of Christian magazines. She has
also compiled the stories in the popular
Winner Books' Animal Tails series: *The
Hairy Brown Angel and Other Animal
Tails; The Peanut Butter Hamster and
Other Animal Tails; Skunk for Rent and
Other Animal Tails; The Incompetent Cat
and Other Animal Tails;* and *The Duck
Who Had Goosebumps and Other Animal
Tails.*

The Pint-sized Piglet

and Other Animal Tails

edited by
GRACE FOX ANDERSON

illustrated by
Janice Skivington Wood

VICTOR BOOKS ®

A DIVISION OF SCRIPTURE PRESS PUBLICATIONS INC.
USA CANADA ENGLAND

"House Tiger," "The Tree-climbing Fox," "Meet the Friendly Hermit Crab," "Tommy Finds a Pet," "Give Me Back My Dog," previously published in *Discovery* by Light and Life Press, Winona Lake, IN 46590. "The Old Turkey Game," previously published in *Reachout* by Light and Life Press. "Laurie's New Friend Midget," "Matt to the Rescue," previously published in *Action* by Light and Life Press. "Forest Carpenter," "Jaws," "Giant of the Sea," "A Desert Ship," "The Fiercest of the Monkeys," previously published in *Story Friends* by the Mennonite Publishing House, Scottsdale, PA 15683. "Jippy, the Lion-hearted," taken with permission from *African Heroes of the Congo Rebellion*, © 1969, published by Africa Inland Mission Press. "Proud as a Peacock," "Tweety Bird," "Strange Animal Partners," "Peanuts," "Wolf Pack," "Wild Colllie of Sawtooth Mountain," and all cartoons, previously published in *Counselor* by Scripture Press Publications, 1825 College Ave., Wheaton, IL 60187. "The Mysterious Mule," "Hideout for a Goat," previously published in *Teen Power* by Scripture Press Publications.

Library of Congress Catalog Card Number: 86-63143
ISBN: 0-89693-480-2

VICTOR BOOKS
A division of SP Publications, Inc.
Wheaton, Illinois 60187

Contents

The Pint-Sized Piglet

~ A TRUE STORY
by Lana Shea

Marie looked over the wooden fence at her family's month-old piglets and laughed with delight. "Oh, Dad," she cried, "isn't that tiny one cute?" The piglets played and squealed as Dad tossed fresh straw into their pen.

"He *is* a cute little guy, but I'm afraid his size is against him," Dad said soberly. "He probably won't make it.

"He's healthy enough now. But because he's a runt, the other pigs will push him away from the food and water. Then he will probably get sick and die."

"That's terrible!" Marie shouted. "Poor little pig!"

She glared angrily at the chubby piglets and saw one of them snap at the reddish-brown "runt," then push him away from the feeder. "Hey, quit that, you meany!" she hollered. She threw a handful of straw at the bully, but the pig ignored her.

"He doesn't know any better, Honey," Dad said as he patted Marie's shoulder. "He just wants to fill his own stomach."

She knew it was natural for animals to be selfish, but she still felt sorry for the runt. She thought about how she felt every time her classmates chose sides for softball. She hated it when she was the last to be picked or when a captain wrinkled her nose and said, "I guess we're stuck with Marie."

Being pushed aside made her feel worthless and sad. But since she had accepted Jesus as her Saviour, she felt better about herself. She knew that if God loved her enough to send Jesus to die for her sins, she must be special to Him. Besides, God had given her loving parents and a big brother who'd stick up for her.

She rested her chin on the wooden fence and gazed down at the little pig, rooting through the straw away from all the others. The poor little fellow didn't have anyone to care for him. Not even a family.

Suddenly, Marie's face brightened. "Dad, I've got it! Why not have a pen just for the runt? Then he could get all the food and water he needs."

"That sounds like a good idea," Dad said. "There's an extra pen I'm not using. But it will take more work to care for just one pig, and I don't have the time."

"Oh, Dad, you won't have to do a thing. I'll take care of him. Can I, please?"

"Well, you *are* 10 years old. The responsibility would be good for you."

Marie's blue eyes widened and she nodded

quickly.

Dad grinned. "OK, he's all yours."

"Oh, boy; oh, boy!" Marie bounced and twirled. The startled piglets jumped and huffed.

"It's OK, little fella. You've got me to take care of you now," Marie told "her" pig.

Marie named her runt Rusty. Soon he would wait for her at the gate of his pen and greet her with hardy grunts. Besides feeding, watering, and cleaning his pen, she always gave him lots of hugs and pats and talked to him every day. She even played Rusty's favorite game of chasing and being chased. She liked being a special friend to the once friendless piglet.

One day while Marie was playing with Rusty, Mom came into the barn. "Marie," Mom said, "Mrs. Mott's granddaughter Tammy is visiting her this week. She wondered if she could come over and play with you today."

Marie groaned. "But, Mom, Tammy's a pain. She's only six, and she never wants to do anything *I* want to. Besides, I wanted to play with Rusty today."

"Maybe Tammy would like to play with Rusty too," Mom suggested.

"Naw, she's a city kid and won't even go into the barn. She says it stinks," Marie said with disgust.

"I understand how you feel," Mom said. "But it won't hurt you to play with Tammy. She gets lonely for someone to play with while she's at her grandma's."

"Oh, OK," Marie grumbled.

Soon Tammy was at the front door with a box of paper dolls. Marie sighed. She really didn't like playing with paper dolls anymore, but she decided to make the best of it.

As they played, Marie told Tammy about Rusty and how the other pigs pushed him away from the feeder. Marie was surprised to see tears well up in Tammy's eyes. "The poor little pig," Tammy said sympathetically. "Why did they do that?"

"Well, I guess it's because they wanted all the food for themselves, and since he was little they could push him around," Marie replied.

"I'm glad you're his friend anyway." Tammy was quiet for a moment, then added, "I wish I lived closer so I could have a good friend like you too."

Tammy's kind words hit Marie hard. She suddenly realized what she had done. When she complained about Tammy coming over, she wasn't a good friend at all. She had been ready to push Tammy away just so she could have the whole day to herself. Marie prayed silently and asked God to forgive her for being selfish.

"Could you show me Rusty?" Tammy asked shyly.

"I thought you didn't like the smell in the barn."

"Well, I don't. But I'd like to be Rusty's friend too. I guess I could put up with the smell," Tammy said, smiling.

"Sure, come on." Marie beamed. She felt good now. Not only had she shared her day with a lonely little girl, but Rusty had found a new friend. He was certainly no longer a "poor little pig."

Tweety Bird

∿ A TRUE STORY
by Delores Elaine Bius

No mistake. Tweety was a sick parakeet and had been for nearly a month. He'd been ill before, but this time he did not seem to respond to 12-year-old Roger's care. Instead, he seemed to get sicker and sicker.

The bright yellow parakeet had entertained the Bius family for five years. He seemed part monkey as he climbed the bars of his cage. He loved to have his tummy rubbed and liked the salt off crackers.

He could say his own name, "Tweety Bird," and the minute anyone came in the door, he would whistle a welcome. He enjoyed music and sang like a canary when the stereo was on.

Every few days Roger would let Tweety out of his cage for flying time. Tweety would swoop around the room, then land on Roger's shoulder. He spent hours chattering to "the other bird" in his cage mirror. He'd even lift the mirror and peek behind it as if in search of that other bird.

Yes, Tweety was a member of the family and was

dearly loved. But his little feet were cold now as he sat fluffed out on his perch next to the heating pad Roger had fastened to one end of the cage.

One afternoon, Roger took Tweety out of the cage. "Do you want to fly, Tweety?" he asked. But the bird only huddled near Roger's neck as if to keep warm, and he wouldn't fly or chirp.

"You seem to be sicker every day," Roger said to his pet. "But I don't like to ask for money to take you to the vet. I know Dad really can't afford it."

But that night at supper, Roger's dad said, "Son, Tweety has been sick nearly a month now, hasn't he? Why don't we take him to a vet tonight?"

"Oh, thanks, Dad," Roger said gratefully. He jumped up and got the phone directory. They found the number of a veterinarian and Roger's mother phoned. The vet told them to bring the bird right in.

They lined a box with a soft towel and made air holes in it, then put Tweety in it.

Dr. Leonas, the veterinarian, examined Tweety Bird and said, "You have a very sick bird here. He has a bad cold, and that is like pneumonia in an old person. I'll give you this medicine—tetracycline. Give him two drops every morning and night. It should help him."

Mr. Bius thought that was quite reasonable. For the next few days, Roger caught Tweety and gave him the medicine with a dropper. After a week and much prayer, Tweety only seemed worse. He made little mewing sounds as if he were in pain.

At breakfast that Saturday, Dad said again, "Son, I think we'd better take Tweety back to the vet this afternoon. I don't like to see him suffer so."

That morning Roger prayed, "God, if Tweety is going to die anyway, please let him die before this afternoon. I hate to see him suffer, and I know Dad can't really afford to pay the vet."

By lunchtime, Tweety was worse but still alive. "Are you sure we should take him in, Dad? He might die anyway," Roger said.

"I know, Son, but at least we'll know we did all we could for him."

Dr. Leonas looked at Tweety and shook his head. "I'm afraid he only has a 50-50 chance. Five years is old for a parakeet. I'm sorry, but you may have to prepare for a funeral."

When Roger's dad went to pay him, Dr. Leonas said, "No. No charge. All we did was talk. Roger, you're a good boy. You like animals, I can tell. When you're older, you can work for me."

Roger smiled and said, "Thanks, Dr. Leonas."

As soon as they got home, Roger opened Tweety's box to put him back in his cage. But the weak little bird was struggling and breathed his last as Roger watched helplessly.

"At least the poor little fellow isn't suffering anymore, Honey," Roger's mother said, in an effort to comfort him.

When Roger could talk again, he said, "Well, Mom, we know we did all we could, as Dad said. And the vet didn't charge anything. So God *did* answer our prayers."

Roger carefully put the little feathered body in a box his mother had lined with paper towels. Then he took it out in the backyard, got a shovel, and buried Tweety.

When he returned to the house, Roger said, "Mom, I wish birds had souls and could go to heaven so I could see Tweety again!"

"I know, Honey," his mother replied. "I guess we should just be grateful that God has provided forgiveness through Jesus for us—so *we* can be with Him in heaven when we die."

"And I guess I can be thankful for the joy Tweety gave us while we had him," Roger said thoughtfully.

Laurie's New Friend Midget

~ A FICTION STORY
by Marge Koenig

Laurie Baldwin sprawled lazily on her bed, dangling a strand of red yarn over the edge. She laughed as two white paws batted the yarn back and forth. The white paws belonged to a small gray cat, lying on its back on the floor and looking for all the world as though the most important matter of the day was getting a grip on that piece of yarn.

Tiring of play, Laurie rolled over on her back. The gray cat jumped up on the bed and curled up beside her, purring. *This is starting out to be a perfect summer,* Laurie thought.

A week ago she had found the cat over on Orchard Road with an injured paw. She had named the cat Midget and cared for it until its paw was better. They were becoming close friends as Laurie learned something new each day about Midget's personality.

"Laurie!" It was Mother. "Hurry and get ready for church now."

In church, Pastor Parsons talked about how giving to others is more meaningful if you give something that is special to you, just as Jesus gave His life for us. Then he asked for volunteers to give some of their time that summer to do odd jobs for the older church members.

When he said "older," Laurie glanced across the aisle at Mrs. Webster, an elderly widow who walked with a cane. She was surprised to see Mrs. Webster wipe a tear from her eye. Laurie looked away quickly, wondering why Mrs. Webster was sad. She didn't like to see people unhappy, especially older people. Then she thought of the pastor's words and knew what she could do.

When the service was over, Laurie went to a sign-up table in the hall. She found Mrs. Webster's name on the list and signed up to weed her flower bed the following Wednesday.

She saw Mrs. Webster then, walking slowly ahead of her with the cane, and decided to tell her when she would be there. But just as Laurie was about to speak, a lady came along and began talking to Mrs. Webster. Laurie could easily hear their conversation.

"Emma," the other woman said, taking Mrs. Webster by the arm, "you look unhappy. Is something wrong?"

"Yes," said Mrs. Webster. "I've lost a very close friend. My dear cat Muffy, who has been at my side for six years, disappeared two weeks ago and I haven't seen her since."

"I'm so sorry, Emma," the other woman said. "What does she look like? Just yesterday I saw a strange black cat near my garage."

"No, Muffy is mostly gray with four white paws and white on her neck and face."

No, no, no! The words screamed in Laurie's head. *It can't be! Midget is MY cat, not hers! It can't be!*

Wednesday came too fast. Laurie wasn't quite as eager to go to Mrs. Webster's house now as she had been on Sunday, but she knew she couldn't break a promise.

Mrs. Webster was expecting her, and after showing her the flower bed that needed weeding, she went inside. Laurie was glad. She would do the weeding quickly—a good job—then go home.

When she finished the job and started walking toward her bike, Mrs. Webster called from the door. "Now, now, you can't leave without proper thanks. I have some freshly baked cookies and lemonade here for both of us."

Laurie stopped, her heart pounding. She could make up a story and tell Mrs. Webster she had to get home right away. But that would be wrong.

"Come along now, Dear—the lemonade is poured."

Laurie slowly followed Mrs. Webster up the steps and inside. The door led right into a large, homey kitchen that smelled like chocolate-chip cookies. It reminded Laurie of her grandmother's home in Pennsylvania. A plate of cookies, still warm from the oven, and two tall glasses of lemonade were waiting on the table by the window.

I'll just finish the cookies and lemonade fast, then leave, Laurie thought to herself. "This is a nice house," she said to Mrs. Webster. "It's something like my grandmother's. Do you live here alone?"

Too late, Laurie realized it was the wrong question.

Mrs. Webster twisted her napkin in her bony fingers. "Well, I guess I do now," she said. "I had a wonderful cat named Muffy until about two weeks ago. She disappeared when a visitor accidentally left the door open. I'm afraid she may have been hit by a car." Mrs. Webster's voice quivered and Laurie saw tears starting to fill her eyes again.

Laurie looked down at her plate. Her stomach felt queasy and she had lost her appetite. She looked around the kitchen for something else to talk about and noticed a basket containing a red cushion and a gray toy mouse. Next to the basket sat two empty dishes with "Muffy" printed on each.

Tears began to fill Laurie's own eyes now. As she turned back to the table, Mrs. Webster was holding out a snapshot. "This is my Muffy," she said.

Through her tears, Laurie saw pictured the gray and white cat she loved. She knew then what she had to do. Jumping up from her chair, Laurie almost knocked it over. "Mrs. Webster," she said, "I have to leave. There's something I have to do."

She bolted out the door, leaving a puzzled Mrs. Webster staring after her.

Five minutes later, Laurie dropped her bike in her own yard and ran into the house. Her mother was in the family room, folding laundry.

"Mom, please help me do something before I lose my courage. Midget can't be mine. Her name is Muffy and she belongs to Mrs. Webster. I love Midget," she sobbed, "but Mrs. Webster needs her more than I do."

Laurie told her mother everything, starting with church on Sunday. Then her mother drove Laurie, with Muffy in her arms, back to Mrs. Webster's. Taking Muffy up to Mrs. Webster's door was the hardest thing Laurie had ever done, but the look on Mrs. Webster's face when she saw Muffy made it less painful.

"Oh, my Muffy, my Muffy!" she exclaimed, taking the cat into her arms. "You're home!"

Laurie brushed a tear from her face and looked up at her mother. Mrs. Baldwin smiled and hugged her close.

Then Laurie told Mrs. Webster about finding Muffy and about overhearing her talking after church. "I almost didn't tell you about Muffy," she added.

"You know, Laurie," Mrs. Webster said, "I think maybe God planned it this way. You took good care of Muffy until her paw was better, and then He led you straight to me. I know how hard it was for you to give her up. I would like it very much if you'd come and visit whenever you want to. I would enjoy your company and you could play with Muffy."

"And I could weed your flower bed and do other things for you too!" Laurie exclaimed, her face brightening.

Mrs. Webster laughed. "Then it's settled. Now let's all go finish the lemonade and cookies. We have a lot to celebrate!"

The Fiercest of the Monkeys

by Gloria A. Truitt

I will not think you're friendly if
    You choose to stare at me.
In fact, I'll throw a stone if I
    Think you're my enemy!
I do not live up high in trees,
    But on the ground I dwell,
Unlike the other monkeys who
    Think treetops are so swell.
I'm loyal to my herd and guard
    My family with great care,
And anyone who comes too close,
    I'll try my best to scare.
I'm quite a favorite at the zoo,
    So on some afternoon
Come watch my silly antics and
    Say, "Howdy, big baboon!"

Just in Time

~ A FICTION STORY
by Betty Steele Everett

Rick pedaled his bike behind his friend Jay as they wove through the big parking lot outside the supermarket. *Sure is hot!* Rick thought. Sweat ran down his face and he was glad for the little breeze he made as he rode.

Suddenly, he heard a low moan or yelp coming from one of the cars he passed. "Wait, Jay!" he called as he turned around and rode back slowly. He peered into the cars nearby. In one, a small black dog lay on the backseat, moaning.

Rick stopped. All the car windows were closed except for an inch or two at the top. The dog was panting hard.

Rick jumped off his bike and tried the car doors. "What are you doing?" Jay asked as he rode up.

"It's too hot for a dog to be shut up in a car!" Rick said. "With the windows closed, a car can get like an oven in no time. The dog could die!"

"But what are you going to do? You better not go

into someone else's car. You could get into trouble."

"I'm just going to roll down the front windows," Rick said, as he opened a door and began to do so. "Why don't you go on to the store and see if you can find the dog's owner."

Rick talked to the dog quietly as he worked. But the animal just lay there. His whole body heaved with every breath. When Rick had put the windows down, he got his water canteen from his bike. "Here, boy," he said gently. There was a dish in the backseat that had had water in it. Rick filled it, then leaned over the back of the front seat to put it down again.

The dog looked up, then saw the water. He moved his head slowly to lap at it.

"Good dog," Rick said.

He was just backing out of the car when a strong hand gripped his shoulder, jerked him out of the car, and spun him around. "Just what do you think you're doing, kid?" a tall young man who was still holding him in a tight grip, demanded.

Rick's heart pounded and his mouth went dry. "I was trying to help your dog. It's too hot in a closed car for an animal."

"I think you were trying to steal him. That's what! Midnight is a valuable dog!"

"But I wasn't!" Rick protested.

A police officer came toward them. "What's the problem?" he asked.

"This kid was in my car, Officer," the young man said, shoving Rick forward. "He was trying to steal my dog. I've only had Midnight a few days and he's worth a lot of money!"

"No!" Rick cried. "I only wanted to help his dog.

My friend will tell you!"

"What friend?" The officer was frowning at him.

Rick looked around desperately, but could not see Jay. What if Jay didn't get back? Where was he? *Please help me, Lord Jesus*, he prayed silently.

"I put water in the dog's dish," Rick said. "Look for yourself."

The young man glanced in the car at the dish. "Not much there. I filled it this morning. You can't lie to me."

"Let's go inside where it's cooler and more private," the officer said.

"But you can't leave Midnight here!" Rick cried. "He'll die in this heat. I read about it in the paper last night. I want to be a vet so I read anything like that about animals."

Just then he remembered. "Here, I cut out the article and put it in my pocket."

Rick pulled the article out and handed it to the officer. The two men looked at it. The dog's owner took the article and read it carefully. "I didn't know this," he muttered. He handed the article back to Rick.

"Maybe I was wrong, Officer," he said. "According to this, the temperature could have gone up to over 150 degrees in there by now! Midnight *could* have died, just as the kid says."

"Maybe I should have waited till my friend found you," Rick said. "He warned me not to open your car, but I was afraid to wait. Your dog was moaning and panting so hard and the water was gone—"

Rick stopped and looked around. "Hey, here

comes my friend now!"

Jay stopped his bike beside them. "What's wrong?" He sounded scared too. "I couldn't find the dog's owner, Rick."

"I own Midnight," the young man said. "And I guess he and I both owe you two our thanks—and an apology. Sorry I got so mad, kid. And thanks, Officer. I guess I was wrong."

The policeman smiled. "Glad it turned out all right. You'd better get some books on how to take care of a dog though, especially if he's as valuable as you say."

"I will."

The officer left, and the young man held out his hand to Rick. "Thanks, kid. No hard feelings?"

Rick grinned. "No hard feelings," he said. "I'm just glad I came along in time to help your pup. He's real cute!"

As the young man got into his car, Jay leaned over and asked quietly, "What happened?"

"I'll tell you about it on the way home," Rick said. "I was really scared, but you know, I'm sure God sent us along just in time."

Hideout for a Goat

~ A FICTION STORY
by Arlene Wolfe

*B*aba Mzee, Baba Mzee!" Liru dashed into the room and stopped in front of his grandfather. "They are going to kill Chelache! I heard them planning."

"What do you say, child? Who's going to kill Chelache? Quit talking like a lion is chasing you." Grandfather tapped his cane and groped with his left hand in the air to touch his grandson.

"I was coming home from our church boys' club by way of the river path. As I neared the Panther Cave, I heard voices, talking secret like! It was some of the Hasha youth warriors."

"They're always starting trouble," Grandfather muttered.

"They said if they were to do their work well, they needed to take an oath and they would need the blood of a goat. Then I heard Kipkobus Ruto—you know him—he lives down by the water mill. He told them I had a goat. I don't want Chelache stolen and I don't want to sell him to anybody who wants to take an oath."

"When those men take an oath, it always means they are planning trouble," Grandfather said.

"The blood of my goat isn't going to be used for that." Liru dramatically stomped his foot. "He's to become your eyes. That is why I've fed and cared for him these past months."

There were few opportunities for making money in Liru's home village near the Zana River in Kenya, Africa. Liru's goat was a prized possession.

"I will be happy to have my eyes," the old man mused. "Chelache is fat enough now to bring us the 40 shillings, just enough for the operation to remove my cataracts. But the market is not until day after tomorrow. Do you think they plan to do something before then?"

"That's what they said. They want to take the oath before Friday. We must think of a place to hide the goat until Friday. He can't stay in the village, for he bleats too much. They would hear him."

"The doctor says I must have the money before he operates. I told him I would have it Friday. We must think." Grandfather slid his hands over his sightless eyes.

"I could try to get a lorry and ride to Murucho to report this to the police, but I have no money nor is there any time," Liru said.

"Where is the goat now?" Grandfather asked.

"Down at the old schoolhouse," Liru answered.

Grandfather whacked the floor with his cane. "Son, are you afraid of evil spirits?"

"Not now that I believe in Jesus."

"But those men are." The old man raised his

head slowly.

"What do you mean?" the boy asked.

"There's an old grove of trees on Ping'ing' Hill with an old witch doctor's hut in the middle of it. No one has lived there this past year. Nobody wants to clear it because it's a spirit grove. Perhaps you could take Chelache there and wait until market day."

"Stay in that hut? Perhaps I could leave Chelache there and just bring him his food."

"Now don't be afraid. It's not as bad as you think. Remember, old Gusomi turned to Christ before he died. He even cleaned up his hut. Of course, it must be dirty by now, but I think it's in good repair. Nobody wants to disturb it because of the old belief."

"Grandfather—" Liru paused. "I think I'll do it. I'll go now, for it's nearly sunset. Good-bye, *Baba Mzee.*"

"You are a brave warrior but a Christian," Grandfather said. "God will be with you and I will see you again with my own eyes."

Liru darted off into the dusk toward the school-house. As he approached the old building, his legs seemed like lead. *What if I'm being followed?* he wondered.

Chelache bleated and his voice sounded so loud in the darkness that Liru jumped. Crawling into the hut, he loosened the goat's rope and gently drew his pet out into the fresh air.

Taking a little-used path, Liru led Chelache silently through the tall elephant grass. The tropical moon had just risen in the east, casting weird shadows upon the path.

Suddenly, Liru saw several men walking toward

him. Automatically, he pushed and pulled his pet behind some rocks. If only they had not been seen! Liru stared at the black boulder in front of him, almost afraid to breathe. He nestled his head next to Chelache.

"Please, God," Liru prayed as he heard the muffled steps of the men on the path a few feet from him, "help the goat keep quiet. Tie up his jaws like you did the lions in the den with Daniel."

When all was quiet again, the boy led his pet onto the path.

In the grove the night bugs sang their endless songs. A mud hen called mysteriously.

Liru's hand trembled as he pushed open the door and drew his goat into the thick darkness. He shuddered as cobwebs tangled against his throat. He brushed them away impatiently. Tying the rope to the window latch, he left his pet in the hut. The door squeaked a ghastly sound as he closed it.

Liru slept restlessly that night in his own hut. At the first streak of dawn, he was up. Chelache would need water and food. Cautiously, he slipped out of the house with a bucket. He could not take a chance of leading Chelache to the river. The river must be brought to him.

Liru worked quickly. The sun rose early at the equator. Dipping his bucket into the river, he rushed up the mountain path. As he neared the hut, he heard Chelache bleat. Was he smart enough to know his master was coming?

"Let's hope no one else enters this grove today," Liru said to himself.

Chelache bleated loudly as Liru opened the

squeaking door. The goat drank the water, and Liru returned to the grove and began cutting some green grass.

All that day Liru herded his uncle's cattle. As he drove them to the river that afternoon, he blew his flute. He had made it at the club meeting. No one else had one like it. Its sound was rather ghostly and weird, but he could play a tune on it.

After driving the cattle back into the kraal for the night, he dashed up the path with his bucket to care for Chelache. He left the water in the darkness of the hut and rushed out into the growing darkness to cut grass.

Suddenly Liru was aware of voices. He was sure one belonged to Kipkobus Ruto.

"I tell you I saw that kid come into this grove with a bucket," Ruto said.

"Aw, I can't believe he would be that brave," commented the other.

"Yah? He is one of those Christians. They do not fear evil spirits. He would know the grove would make a good hiding place for his goat."

"Do you think someone told him?"

"Yes, I do."

"We must have that goat for our oath. If we take a goat from one of the old men, they'll report us to the *serkali,* but Liru is just a boy. Nobody will listen to him. His old grandfather is almost blind."

"Eee! He's too old to say anything. And Liru's uncle has gone to the capital for several days. We must find that goat tonight."

"Ah—ah—" The voice stopped. "Are you willing to go into the grove?"

"Why not? Gusomi has been dead for months and nothing has happened," Ruto said.

"Yes, but—"

"Are you a coward? I shall report you to the Hasha Warriors. Come!"

Liru heard the footsteps of the men enter the trees. What could he do? There were two of them. Was he to lose his goat just the day before it was sold? His hands dropped to his sides. He stood rigid. Suddenly, he was aware of his flute in his pocket. The flute—its eerie sound—it was worth a try.

Crouching in the shadow of some rocks, he began to play long quivery tones up and down the scale. Through the bushes, he saw the men stop. Liru almost gasped in fright. What if they came to investigate?

But the men took a step backward. A blast of wind shook the trees and carried the flute tones throughout the grove. The men dropped their walking sticks and sprinted out of the grove over the side of the hill. Liru continued to blow on his flute.

Finally too tired to blow any longer, he sank against the rock and rested. When it was completely dark, he crawled from his hiding place with his bundle of grass. The goat was safe. He was sure the men would not return. Chelache would be sold tomorrow, and Grandfather would see again.

Liru bowed his head and whispered, "Thank You, God."

A Desert Ship

by Gloria A. Truitt

I carry nomads on my back
　　Across the desert sands,
While eating thorny, spiny plants
　　That grow in arid lands.
I drink a lot of water, and
　　A great deal I can store
Within my body while I work—
　　A week and sometimes more!
I carried the three wise men too...
　　I'm quite a famous mammal!
I'm sometimes called a *desert ship*,
　　But usually, a camel!

Genesis 24:19

Proud as a Peacock

~ A NATURE STORY
by Grace Helen Davis

Among the most beautiful birds in the world is the large, showy peacock. The peacock, or male peafowl, is about as big as a turkey.

He is outstanding in any zoo because of his richly colored feathers. The Indian peacock is the most common kind. His wings are greenish blue and purplish blue. They're tipped with copper.

Actually the peacock's beautiful "tail" or train, sometimes five or six feet long, isn't a tail at all. Rather it is an extension of the back feathers.

The shorter, true tail is made of stiff quills. It holds up the long train feathers so the peacock can raise or lower them as he wishes.

The beautiful train is green with large patterned "eyes" ringed with blue and bronze.

The peahen, or female peafowl, is smaller than the cock. Her colors are mostly browns and dull white, with some green. Her tail is deep brown with white tips.

Other peafowl may be blue, green, or white.

Peacocks have always interested people. During Solomon's time, "every three years once came the ships of Tarshish bringing gold, and silver, ivory, and apes, and peacocks" (2 Chronicles 9:21).

The Greeks and Romans regarded peacocks as sacred, partly because of the "eyes" in their trains. Others valued the peacock as a fancy lawn decoration or for his tasty meat.

But today most peacocks live only in zoos. They are noisy, hard to raise, and ready to fight. They don't have to be around very long before it is obvious that their great beauty doesn't make up for their bad dispositions.

Sometimes boys and girls who are attractive or have expensive clothes think they "have it made." They strut around like peacocks, thinking people will like them no matter how selfish and disagreeable they are.

What a mistake! A girl or fellow who is admired only for his or her looks can never be sure of having true, faithful friends. Of course, all of us want to be attractive. But it takes more than outward beauty to achieve that.

We need an inner, God-given beauty as well. That's the only kind that is real and lasting! Remember that man looks on the outside, but God looks at our hearts—our thoughts and behavior (1 Samuel 16:7).

Jippy, the Lion-Hearted

～ A TRUE STORY
by Harold Olsen

The Simbas are headed this way!" Mr. Brashler cried as he rushed into the house one day. "It isn't safe for us to stay here on the mission station. We must leave as soon as we can get our belongings together!"

It was 1964. A revolution had broken out in the Congo (now Zaire) in Africa. The Simbas were rebels who dressed like lions and were attacking and murdering whole villages. Missionaries especially were in danger.

As the Brashlers loaded their car, Stevie Brashler's large dog, Jippy (a dog bred to hunt lions), came running up. "We're taking Jippy, aren't we, Dad?" Stevie pleaded.

Mr. Brashler shook his head. "I'm sorry, Stevie. We don't know where we may have to go. It would be better for Jippy to stay here."

Modeste Chacu, one of the Brashler's workmen, was helping them put things in the car. "I'll take good care of Jippy," he said. "Don't worry about him."

A few days after the Brashlers left, the Simbas reached the Rethy station. Modeste and the other Africans at the station soon realized their lives were in danger too. Modeste and his brother Simon decided to try to escape to the neighboring country of Uganda.

The two young men got on bicycles and called to Jippy. They were pedaling hard down a back road when, suddenly, three Simbas leaped out at them, screaming and waving spears. Modeste turned just in time to see a Simba thrust his spear through Simon. "O God, help me!" Modeste cried as another rebel lifted his spear to kill him.

Jippy, usually a gentle dog, leaped growling at the throat of Modeste's attacker.

The armed rebel jumped out of the way just in time. "Let's get out of here!" he cried. "That dog will kill us." And the three armed men ran off down the road.

Modeste turned to his brother, but seeing that he was dead, got back on his bicycle. "Come, Jippy," he called. "We can't help Simon now. We've got to hurry." Obediently, the big dog came running and stayed by Modeste until they reached safety.

When the Brashlers returned to the Congo, Modeste gladly told them how, instead of him taking care of Jippy, God had used the dog to save Modeste's life.

"O Jippy," Stevie cried, hugging his furry friend, "I'm glad now that we left you behind. You were like one of God's guardian angels to Modeste."

Tommy Finds a Pet

~ A FICTION STORY
by Ingram See

Tommy knew he could not have a dog. But he couldn't keep from asking again. He ran straight to the kitchen when he came home from school.

"Mom, we all have to take pets for our pet fair next Friday at school, so I *have* to have a dog."

"Here are cookies fresh from the oven, Tommy," his mother said. She moved her sewing machine and something that looked as if it were going to be a shirt from the table to a shelf in the corner. She set a plate of cookies in front of him and poured milk into his mug. Mom knew all about feeding boys.

He grabbed a cookie and took a big bite. "Everybody else will have a pet, so—" He stopped until he could swallow.

"Everybody, Tommy?" Mom asked. "Even the children who live in small apartments?"

Nine-year-old Tommy started to drink his milk. He didn't want to talk about the children who were going to bring posters and drawings instead of live pets. Finally he said, "But Brad will take his collie." (Brad, next door, was his best friend.) "It's not fair if I can't have one too—just a little dog."

Mom put the milk back in the refrigerator. "You can have anything small enough to be kept in a cage, Tommy. You know that. A bird or a gerbil or—"

"Aw, birds and gerbils can't play with you. They don't love you!"

Mom sat down in the chair across the table. "Someday, Tommy, we'll have a house and yard big enough for you and Dan to have dogs." Dan was his older brother.

But Tommy wanted a dog now. He thought of next Friday when all his friends would have their pets at school. He finished his milk and felt his eyes watering. He grabbed up the last two cookies. "You'll be sorry!"

He ran out the front door and across the little yard. He looked back and saw his mother watching him through the screen door. Well, he'd show her. He knew where he could hide. Then she would be so worried she'd let him have a dog.

Tommy kicked a stone along the sidewalk. He knew how to get into that old vacant house at the next corner. Somebody had broken the basement door open. He kicked the stone into the street as he crossed at the corner.

He saw a bus stopping. His father might be coming home on it. He hurried and ran into the big yard by the empty house.

"Tommy!" he heard.

Oh, oh! That was Dad.

"Don't go into that vacant house!" Dad knew all

about keeping boys safe.

Tommy stopped, turned from the house, and walked over to the bushes by the fence. He saw a lot of fallen leaves on the bushes. "I'm looking—for leaves, Dad!" he called, remembering they had to take colored leaves Monday for their October art project.

Tommy picked up a yellow leaf, and Dad went on home. He'd better not go into the empty house now. Well, he would just walk and walk, far away from home.

As he picked up a twig with a red leaf on it, he saw a funny little creature sitting on the twig. It was about four inches long with a triangle-shaped head and big eyes.

It turned its little head like a person and looked over its shoulder at him. It had to be an insect for it had six legs. Its wings were resting on its sticklike body.

"What're you doing here?" That was his brother Dan cutting across the yard from the junior high in the block behind.

"What's this funny bug, Dan? It's looking at me."

Dan picked up the twig and the bug turned and looked at him. "It's a praying mantis. She's looking for flies or moths to eat. See how big her abdomen is? She's got a case of eggs inside her."

Dan knew all about insects. He had a collection of butterflies and beetles mounted on poster board on the wall of their room.

"Will she lay the eggs right there?"

"If she doesn't starve to death first." The mantis started to crawl toward Dan's hand, and he laid the twig down on the bushes again. "She ought to be near garbage cans with flies, but she's getting too heavy to fly much." Dan turned and walked on toward home.

Tommy waved a finger back and forth in front of the mantis. *I must start walking,* he reminded himself. *I'm going miles and miles from home.* But he couldn't keep from watching the mantis. She was looking at his finger and crawling toward it. When he pulled his hand back, she looked up at him with her big eyes. She looked as if she were asking him for help.

"Dan!" he called. "Can I feed her?" He didn't want her to starve to death.

"Sure!" Dan slowed and called back. "Put her in that large peanut butter jar I have with the screen-covered lid, and get her some live flies and moths." Dan hurried on because he played football after school.

Tommy held out his hand again, and the mantis crawled onto it. Then he began walking slowly toward home. He didn't want to scare her. By the time he reached home, she was climbing up his arm. So he bent his elbow and lifted it, and the mantis turned around and began crawling back toward his hand.

"I'm going to name you Monkey because you like to climb so much," he told her.

By the time he reached his and Dan's room, she was resting on his finger up in the air. While he was getting Dan's screen-topped jar out of the closet, Dan came in eating a cookie and began changing his shoes. "Put in some sticks for her to lay her egg case on," Dan said as he picked up his helmet and ran out the door.

With Monkey still on his finger, Tommy took the jar out to the bush by the front steps so he could get some twigs off the bush. He broke off a twig and held it out to Monkey and watched her crawl onto it. He laid the stick with Monkey on it on the walk by his feet. "Don't fly away, Monkey," he said.

He began breaking sticks off the bush. When he looked down, Monkey was right there looking up at him. He picked up the jar and took off the lid. Then he pulled off the leaves still hanging on the sticks so they were smooth. One stick was too long. He broke it so it would fit in the jar. He placed the sticks so Monkey could climb up in any direction.

As he finished, Brad came running over from his house with his collie. "What're you doing, Tom?"

"Hey, don't step on Monkey!" Tommy looked down. Monkey was not there. He looked all around. She wasn't on the walk or the steps. He looked at the bush and at the grass, but she was greenish brown, and he wouldn't be able to see her on the bush or the grass.

"Don't step on what?" Brad started looking too.

Tommy didn't answer. He was sure Brad had never seen a bug look at you as if it were begging you to help it.

Suddenly Brad stretched out his hand toward Tommy's shoulder. "Hey, swat that off!"

Tommy looked down at his own shoulder. There was Monkey. She had climbed up his shoe to his jeans to his jacket. He put his hand up and Monkey crawled on it. He put his hand down into the jar, she crawled off onto a stick, and he put the lid on. "She's my pet, Brad," he said as Brad and his collie ran off around the house. "Don't scare the flies from the garbage can."

Tommy took the jar into his and Dan's room and got out Dan's butterfly net. In the kitchen, Mom stopped him. "Would you take this out to the garbage can, Tommy?" She pointed to a bag of peelings and stuff on the sinkside.

"OK, Mom. I'm going for food for Monkey anyway."

"A monkey?" Mom said. "But, Tommy, you know we don't even have room for a kitten—"

"Mom!" He laughed at his mother. "Monkey is here in the jar. See? She's a mantis—my new pet." Then he laughed at himself. "Maybe Monkey just likes to climb," he said. "But she acts as if she really and truly likes me."

"WHY COULDN'T SHE HAVE HAD HER KITTENS IN A DRESSER DRAWER?"

Matt to the Rescue

~ A FICTION STORY
by Bobbie Montgomery

S on, hop on your bike. Go down to the
hardware store and buy some nails for me. Here's a
sample of what I want," Dad said.

Matt shoved the nail and money into his pocket
while heading for his bike.

He breathed deeply of the morning air as he
pedaled along and thought about Monday. He had to
write a story for English about a wild animal or a
pet. He didn't have any pets, so he supposed he'd
have to write a poky old story without any
adventure.

Just as he went around the corner, his wheel
caught in the grate covering the storm sewer where
water went when it rained. He could see the black-
ness and thick mud through the spaces in the grate
as he pulled his back wheel loose.

If I were very small, he thought, *that would
seem like the deep pit the Bible tells about—the one
they put Jeremiah in.*

45

Matt went into the hardware store and bought the nails. Coming out, he glanced up the street. An old, battered car pulled up at the corner where he had caught his wheel in the grate. A man climbed out of the car, and a big yellow cat hopped out after him.

What is he doing? Why, he's dropping something down through the grate, Matt realized.

The man got back into the car and drove away. "He left the cat!" Matt exclaimed out loud. Matt wheeled around and quickly pedaled back to where the cat was running wildly around the grate, and meowing.

Matt parked his bike and peered through the grate. He could see two tiny kittens squirming around in the mud and water of the storm sewer.

What a cruel man, to poke kittens down there! The poor mama cat wanted her babies. What should he do? He pulled on the grate, but he couldn't move it.

He glanced up and noticed a police car coming slowly toward him. Policemen were supposed to help. Matt ran out into the street, waving his arms.

The car eased over to the curb and the officer asked, "What's the matter?"

Matt sputtered. "A man stuffed some kittens down the drain. They belong to that mama cat."

A grim expression came over the officer's face. He climbed out of his car and looked the situation over. He got a wrench from his car and pried the grate up. "There they are, kid. Think you can reach them if I hang onto you?"

"I think so," Matt replied.

The officer got a firm grip on Matt's ankles and helped him down into the darkness, head first. It was black, scary, and damp. His head felt like a balloon being blown up.

The kittens kept trying to get away from him. He grabbed one, but it was slippery with slime and slithered away, yowling in fright. Matt managed to get the other one by the front leg. It didn't try to get away. It was very quiet.

Skinning his arm on a rock and splashing some of the mud on himself, he made a dive for the other one.

"Hey!" the officer yelled as he let one of Matt's feet slip, but quickly grabbed it again. "OK?" he asked.

"Yeah, I got them," Matt yelled, and the officer pulled him slowly back onto the street.

The mother cat ran frantically around Matt, trying to get near her babies. He held the lively one down to her, and she started cleaning it with her tongue. The officer helped her by wiping some of the mud away with a piece of newspaper he found nearby.

Matt looked at the one in his arms. It didn't move or cry.

The officer stood up. He felt the kitten Matt had. "Sorry, son; it's dead. It was probably weak when he threw it in the drain." He wrapped it in some of the newspaper and put it in the back of his car.

Matt felt sad about the dead kitten. "That was the meanest man I've ever seen," he said. He picked up the mother cat and held the kitten close to her. Mama and kitten seemed happy to be together.

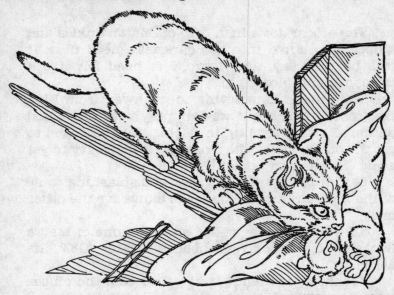

Glaring down the street, Matt said, "How could he do that?"

The officer shook his head. "Some people just don't have a heart for animals," he said. "Now that you saved the kitten, what will you do with it and the mother?"

"Take them home, I guess," Matt said. "Mom and Dad are pretty good about animals. They'll want to help them when I tell what happened. Mom and Dad would never be mean to God's creatures."

"OK, you climb in the front seat with your cats, and I'll put your bike in the trunk; then I'll take you home," the officer said.

Matt held the mother cat close, and the kitten cuddled near her. When they drove into the driveway, Dad stuck his head out of the garage in surprise.

Mother came running from the house calling, "What happened, Matt?"

"Everything's OK, Ma'am," the officer said, and told them about the rescue.

Mother got a box and put an old piece of blanket into it for a bed.

Matt put a bowl of milk in front of the mother cat. She lapped up the milk quickly. Then she lifted the kitten in her mouth and jumped into the box.

The officer asked Matt what the man looked like who dumped the cats and what kind of car he drove.

"I'm glad it was Matt who saw them," he said as he left. "He's a good boy."

"That he is," Dad said, as they watched the police car disappear. Then he turned to Matt. "By the way, where are my nails?"

Matt grinned and got the nails out of his bike carrier. "Here they are, Dad. I can keep the cats, can't I?"

Dad put his arm across Matt's shoulder. "I guess so. I did tell you that you could have a pet. Just get out of those muddy clothes and go take a shower."

"In just a minute," Matt said. He had to have one last look at his pets. His mother was wiping the kitten off some more with a wet cloth. It was going to be fluffy and yellow like its mother.

Matt stooped over and patted the mama cat. She looked up at him and started purring.

"Boy, have I ever got an animal story to write for English class now!" Matt exclaimed. "I'll name the kitten and the story *Jeremiah,* because I got the little thing out of a dark, muddy pit." (See Jeremiah 38:1-13.)

The Tree-Climbing Fox

~ A NATURE STORY
by Mary Emma Allen

Foxes often earn a bad name because they like to eat hens and young chicks and other young birds. But actually, the gray fox is one of God's more interesting creatures. And he does some good by eating insects, rats, and mice that harm farm crops.

The gray fox is different from his relative, the red fox, because he can climb trees to escape enemies and find food. God has given him long, sharp claws, especially the back claws.

He climbs by grasping the tree with his front feet and using them somewhat like hands and digging his back claws in to push himself up the tree, much as a boy shinnies up. Once up, he will even walk out on a branch.

The gray fox lives all over the United States in swamps and woodlands, and also in thickets in the desert. He is shy and smaller than the red fox.

This interesting animal has salt-and-pepper colored fur and a black mark along the top of a rather bushy tail. Along the sides of his neck, underneath his body, and on his legs, he is rust-colored.

Gray foxes are members of the canine or dog family. We don't see them often because gray foxes are *nocturnal* (night) creatures. They hunt for food mainly at night and hide or sleep during the day.

Their dens are usually in small caves or hollow logs, but sometimes they'll use an old woodchuck burrow. They've even been known to make themselves at home in old cemeteries, under a barn, or in hollows near a roadway. But usually they stay far from people.

The young fox pups are born in the spring and come out of the dens in May or June. The fox family will stay together all summer. The mother, or sometimes the father, teaches the young how to catch mice (their favorite food) and insects, and look for berries. The mother is very patient with them while they're learning and takes care of her young for four months, longer than most other wild animals.

During the day, the pups may come out of the den to romp and play. Like young puppies, they frisk about and are fun to watch if you ever have a chance. But don't ever pick up a fox, not even a pup, because foxes are one of the most common carriers of rabies.

Even though the gray fox may be a pest at times, it is only because he is hunting for food, following his natural instincts. Generally the gray fox is more helpful than harmful because of his importance in the balance of nature. He reminds us of God's many wonders in this world and that all things are "of Him, and through Him, and to Him" (Romans 11:36).

House Tiger

by Jacqueline Rowland

He stalks through the house—
   His whiskers aquiver!
The gleam in his eye
   Would make a mouse shiver!

Then leaps in wild frenzy,
   His claws find a place
For climbing and scratching
   Our curtains of lace.

Sometimes he takes time out
   To purr and to doze;

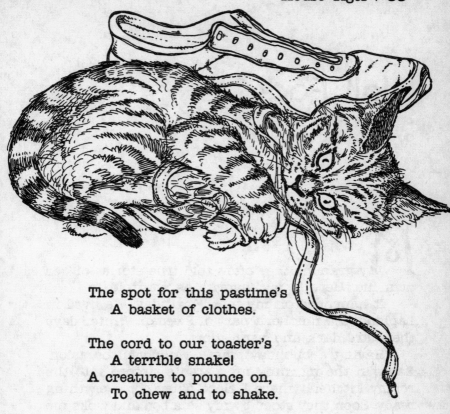

The spot for this pastime's
    A basket of clothes.

The cord to our toaster's
    A terrible snake!
A creature to pounce on,
    To chew and to shake.

He'll sit on a shoulder,
    But just when he wishes—
His favorite time
    Is when we do the dishes.

He's too silly and foolish
    To capture a mouse;
And yet this small tiger—
    Is king of the house!

Wolf Pack

~ A TRUE STORY
by Thyra Wickman

My grandmother often told true stories of her own life. Here is my favorite as she told it:

It happened on my tenth birthday. We lived in Lapland, the northern part of Sweden. Winter days there are dark and very short.

Having a birthday was a wonderful occasion. Early in the morning my parents tiptoed into the roomy kitchen, where I slept. They got everything ready. Soon they stood by my sofa bed and woke me by singing a beautiful hymn. Mother then brought me a tray with food and lighted candles on it. Father came behind her, holding gifts.

That day I received a woolen stocking cap with a great big tassel. There was also a sled—one that Father had made for me.

Before Father left for work, we worshiped God in prayer as we did every morning. Because it was my birthday, the Bible verse for the day was dedicated to me. Father read it from the large family Bible:

"He shall call upon Me, and I will answer him; I will be with him in trouble; I will deliver him, and honor him" (Psalm 91:15).

It did not take me long to put on my new stocking cap and try out my sled. All morning I slid on the lake below our house. That afternoon I tried the long slope down the mountainside.

I struggled up the mountain road with my sled. Though it was only 2 o'clock, darkness was stealing over the forest. I had almost reached the top when I heard a fearful noise. Anyone in Lapland would know that howl. Wolves! A pack of them. They must have been hungry to come near our homes before dark.

Before I could turn my sled around, I saw them. There must have been six or eight wolves. They ran at lightning speed. In a minute they would be upon me.

As I threw myself on the sled, I remembered the Bible verse of the morning. I called on the Lord God with all my heart and soul. I did not know just how—but I knew that He could deliver me from those hungry beasts.

The sled sped faster and faster down the hill. I could hear the wolves not far behind. At my speed I would coast across most of the lake. I did not dare to think any further.

As I crossed the lake, the answer to my prayer came. I heard a loud crash and splash.

When Mother found me a little later, I was still lying on my sled. The shock had been too much for me. I had fainted. She bent over and patted my cheek.

"You are a lucky, lucky girl," she said. "Those

wolves fell into the ice hole your father cut last night. Right now they are all down on the bottom of the lake."

But my heart knew it was not luck. My God had answered my prayer. And all these years since, He has answered my prayers and taken care of me.

Giant of the Sea
(The Largest Creature that Ever Lived)

by Gloria A. Truitt

The greatest dinosaur that lived
    Was not as big as me.
I'm bigger than ten elephants!
    My home is in the sea!
Unlike my neighbors, I breathe air...
    I'm not a fish at all...
And I can even make a sound
    Just like a *mooing* call!
I surface when I want to breathe...
    My vapor I exhale
Through two nostrils on my head
    Because I am a whale!

The Day Duncan Disappeared

〜 A FICTION STORY
by Irma Wallem

When anyone in my family calls me Elizabeth, I know my rat, Duncan, has done something just awful, like getting into the dish-towel drawer or leaving little black pellets around the kitchen floor where my sister goes barefoot to sneak chocolate ice cream at night.

It does not seem to matter to anyone that Duncan, who was born in the Smithville High School science laboratory, is mine only by a twist of fate. I say fate, because my sister Karen, who is 15—5 years older than I am—does not care to be seen with me, except on rare occasions.

It was the last day of school. Just as I entered the science room, I heard Mr. Reese, the teacher, call out to the departing students, "Anybody want to take home this white rat? He can't stay here all summer."

Strange to say, no one stepped forward. Several of the boys snickered and I heard one say, "Not me, man, what do I want with a rat?"

I walked over to the cage and stood there while Karen got her books together. Mr. Reese found a shoe box and punched some holes in the top, put Duncan in, and handed the box to me without a word. My expression must have told him how much I wanted that rat.

Karen, who is dark like my father's side of the family, sometimes tries to give the impression that I don't belong to her.

She took off toward home a couple of steps ahead of me, but I talked to her anyway. "I promise to keep my white rat in the backyard in Peter's cage," I said. Peter was my pet rabbit who got away when I forgot to latch the cage door.

Mom saw us coming and opened the front door with a welcoming smile, until Karen gave her one of those meaningful looks in the direction of my shoe box. Mom stopped smiling. "What is it this time?" she asked.

Karen shrugged. "Don't blame me, even if my teacher did give it to her. The rats were a scientific experiment and all the rest of them died."

"I'll put him outside in Peter's cage," I said, leaving the two of them to talk about me, as usual.

The next day I hit on a really clever name for my new pet. Once I had heard Mom say that if I had been a boy, she would have named me Duncan. That was her last name before she married Dad.

After that, I spent a lot of time outdoors, talking to Duncan through his wire cage. Then I experimented and found that if I took him out and put him on my shoulder, he would not try to jump down. He

would curl his pink tail around my neck and snuggle
his nose under my ear.

Summers can be kind of lonely with so many
kids off at camp or on vacations. I spent a lot of time
with Duncan. Every day it was harder to leave him
in his cage.

"You might as well bring Duncan onto the service porch," Mom conceded one day. "He can't do
much damage there."

On the service porch there was nothing except a
stack of old newspapers, a clothes hamper, and the
washer and dryer. I fixed Duncan a bed of old rags in
a shoe box in the corner and sometimes he lay in it.
But more often he snuggled on top of the washing
machine.

One day when the washer was going jump-jump,
I set him back on the lid just to see what he would
do.

Instead of jumping to the floor, he rode it, just
like a bucking bronco. I called Mom and Karen and
they both laughed. I told several of my girlfriends
about the way Duncan rode the washer and they
asked when our next washday would be so they
could come and watch him.

However, Karen never invited any of her friends
to the service porch. One day I heard her complain-
ing to Mom that some of her friends referred to me
as "that sister of yours with a rat."

One afternoon Karen acted more uptight than
usual. She was going to have her first date with
Weldon Smith. She tried on three pairs of jeans and
four sweaters, trying to decide which was the most
delapidated. She had just settled on the green sweat-

er with the hole in the sleeve when Weldon came to the door. I let him in and he stood by the sofa looking uncomfortable. Suddenly Duncan scurried in and almost ran over Weldon's foot. He jumped, then laughed.

That would have been a perfect time for Karen to laugh too. But no, she glared at me and flounced out the door. Weldon followed her, but the two of them did not look very friendly as they rode off on their bikes.

"Don't mind my sister," I comforted poor Duncan. I put him in my lap and settled down to watch cartoons on TV. I guess I must have dozed, for the next thing I knew I was awakened by a scream from the kitchen.

I ran out there as fast as I could. Mom stood there by the door. She had stopped screaming and was laughing instead.

"I just caught sight of Duncan's tail sticking out from under the door and thought it was Cecil, come back to haunt me," she said. Cecil was my pet garter snake who went down the drain when I tried to give him a bath.

"I'm sorry," I told Mom. "I'll put Duncan in his box on the porch and won't let him in the house again." I really meant it.

Next day, Karen still seemed on edge. Her date must not have gone the way she planned. Whenever she caught sight of me, she looked the other way, as if I were too awful to endure.

She made me feel so depressed, I decided to go get a little love and affection from Duncan. He was not in his box. I moved the clothes basket and looked

under the washer and dryer. Then I saw that someone had left the screen door, leading to the outside
world, ajar just a little. Remembering how Cecil had
escaped through a hole smaller than he was, I was
sure Duncan had escaped through the crack in the
door.

Outdoors, I searched under bushes, in flower
beds, and along the picket fence. Then I began to cry.
I went into the front room and found Karen there,
reading a book, as if nothing had happened. "I hope
you're satisfied now," I sobbed. "It was probably you
who left the screen door unlatched on purpose."

Mom came hurrying into the living room. "She
didn't mean to let him out—if he is out," she said.
"Let's look some more inside."

Karen put a bookmark in the book she was
reading and got up slowly. "He might have gone
upstairs," she said. "I'll look for him when I gather
up my clothes to wash."

"I'll look in all the kitchen drawers," Mom said.
"And, Karen, when you wash your things, you might
as well get the dirty clothes from the hamper and do
a full load."

Remembering how Duncan might never be
around to ride the washer like a bucking bronco
again, I started to cry. He might never again curl his
little pink tail around my neck or snuggle under my
ear. I went outside to look some more, but my heart
wasn't in it. I had almost lost hope.

I returned to the porch at last and there was
Karen, flouncing to the washer with her armload of
dirty clothes. She dumped them into the machine
and started the water going.

"Don't forget the clothes in the hamper," I reminded her.

She picked up the hamper and dumped the clothes in without sorting them. Then she put down the lid.

"You forgot the soap!" I yelled.

She opened the lid and began to scream. I ran to look.

There was poor little pink-all-over Duncan with his wet fur looking matted and gray. He was letting out little squeaks.

"You tried to drown him!" I cried.

Mom came running. She looked down into the washer and began to laugh. I grabbed Duncan and a dry towel, and rubbed his fur.

"We should have guessed he could open the clothes hamper and crawl in for a nap," Mom said.

"He's an educated rat."

All of a sudden Karen began to laugh too. "Yes, he is educated," she said. "High school."

I held Duncan up against me in his towel, but then I reached over and patted Karen's arm. She even bent down and gave me a quick kiss on the forehead, with her eyes shut, probably so she wouldn't have to see Duncan.

In a little while, he was as cute as ever—and cleaner.

The Mysterious Mule

~ A TRUE STORY
by Anna C. Atwood

We were living in a town called Santa Rosa de Copan in the little Republic of Honduras in Central America. One day my husband and I, who were missionaries, were asked to open a church which had been closed for nearly a year. Since the church was in another village, Dulce Nombre, that meant we would have to move.

We believed God wanted us to make this move, but it seemed impossible from our viewpoint. My husband had a blood clot in his leg. It was very painful when he lowered his foot to the floor. I could pack and move small things, but what about the large, heavy items such as furniture?

Just when we were most puzzled, Ricardo Jimenez came our way. Another missionary had sent him to Dulce Nombre to buy a mule named Chocolate. But when he reached the town, Chocolate had vanished. We met Ricardo as he was walking the long distance back home. "Come and stay with us

65

until the mule is found," we suggested.

While Ricardo waited, he built a small platform on wheels where my husband could be placed on his chair with his leg up. While my husband directed the packing, Ricardo and I took orders. We scurried here and there following his directions. All the time I worked I worried that the mule would reappear and we would lose Ricardo's good help.

Each day we got word from Dulce Nombre that the owners were searching high and low for the mule, but he was still missing.

"Why can't Ricardo help us move to Dulce Nombre?" my husband asked. "After all, that is where the mule lives."

So Ricardo kindly lifted all our heavy things into a large truck we rented. After the long trip over mud roads, which would soon be unusable because of rains, we arrived after dark at Dulce Nombre.

I heaved a sigh of relief. Here we were and Ricardo was still with us to help. But what if Chocolate turned up in the morning? Ricardo wouldn't be there to help set up my sink or arrange the furniture.

Shining my flashlight over the doors and windows of the old house, I saw with dismay that the woodwork was badly eaten by termites. *Oh,* I thought wistfully, *Ricardo is such a good carpenter. If only the mule could stay lost, Ricardo might be able to fix all this for us.*

For once in my life, I prayed that something lost might stay lost a little while longer. When morning came, the mule was still missing. By now I was very fond of the mischievous animal.

Ricardo pushed all the heavy furniture in place as I indicated. Then he set up my sink in the kitchen. Afterward, he repaired the windows and doors. He stayed two days, helping us in every way possible.

The next morning, when everything was in good order, we heard a noise at the door. I expected to find a neighbor or a beggar when I opened it. But guess what I found? There stood Chocolate, rubbing his nose against the door. The former owner of this house had fed the mule at this door years before, we discovered later.

We all looked at each other, grinning. "Well," announced Ricardo, "I guess I must go now. My ride is here."

"THE AUDIENCE IS WAITING FOR YOU TO SIT ON YOUR BOX. CAN'T YOU READ AFTER THE SHOW?"

Strange Animal Partners

~ A NATURE STORY
by Billie Avis Chadwick

I f a bird, a crab, an ant, or a wasp said, "Meet my business partner," you would probably look around for another bird, crab, ant, or wasp. But instead you would be introduced to an entirely different kind of creature. Some of the strangest partnerships in the world are among our friends in the animal world.

One of the most amazing teams lives on the floor of the ocean. In this briny partnership there is one bossy character who seems to sit back and give the orders.

Known as the sea anemone, he is a lazy animal that loafs around among the rocks, looking pretty. He has brilliantly colored tentacles that float with the movement of the water like the petals of a flower. And he looks much like a flower. When he gets hungry, he sends his partner, the damselfish, out for some fast food.

Now going after food is dangerous for the little damselfish. It has to swim out among the big fish, and hang around until one of them decides the damselfish would make a nice meal. Then the damselfish darts back to its flowerlike partner, making sure the enemy is in hot pursuit.

If the damselfish makes it home, it swims over the sea anemone, who reaches out an innocent-looking "petal," taps the enemy, paralyzing him, then he and the damselfish share him.

Sometimes, however, the "food" is too "fast" and the damselfish ends up inside him, instead. When that happens, the sea anemone may still come out the winner, for the large fish, now well-fed and happy, may see him and come to figure out what this bright colored "flower" is. In that case, the flowerlike creature snatches him.

Now, of course, the anemone must find a new partner. That means keeping his eyes open for another brave damselfish who is a fast swimmer.

Satan, like the sea anemone, is always looking for new partners. He attracts kids with promises that sound big, important, and desirable. He says, "Team up with me and I'll help you be popular and look mature." He makes smoking and drinking and popping pills look big—until you get hooked on them. But he doesn't care what they do to you—just like the sea anemone when the big fish swallows his partner.

If no damselfish is interested in becoming the sea anemone's second partner, a hermit crab may answer the ad. The hermit crab is a rascal who likes nothing better than a quarrel. He will pick a fight with his own mother over a choice bit of food even after just finishing a huge meal.

But he has to be careful when fighting to keep his tail protected. His shell doesn't cover his tail. If an enemy bites him in his bare spot, it will kill him. So the hermit crab must protect himself. Sometimes he makes a deal with an anemone. The flowerlike animal sits on the crab's back, protects his tail, and gets a free ride. The anemone also helps him kill his prey and shares the food.

If the hermit crab can't find an anemone to sit on him, he will find a discarded shell for his protection. Sometimes a young sponge rides on the shell, giving the crab added protection. As the sponge grows larger, surrounding the shell, he leaves a channel or tunnel for the crab to go in and out. Later, the crab invites a worm to come and share the tunnel and eat the garbage.

The shark sucker is a salt-water creature who teams up with any one of several unwilling partners. Apparently he is too lazy to move through the ocean on his own power, so he attaches himself to a shark, a turtle, a whale, or a large fish, hanging on by means of a sucker disk on his back.

If no live creature is handy, the shark sucker will attach himself to a boat. He doesn't seem to mind who his partner is as long as he gets a free ride to his next meal. And he is protected from enemies when he is with a bigger companion.

One time a shark was captured with four of these unwanted hitchhikers attached to his body. As soon as the shark was lifted from the water, the suckers let go and disappeared in the ocean. They didn't want to be around when trouble came.

Have you ever known a kid who acted like a

shark sucker? Mike was one of these. He attached himself to Phil, who was good in sports. Mike wanted others to see him with Phil because Phil was popular.

But when Phil, a Christian, stood up for an unpopular boy in school and the other kids turned against him, Mike dropped him too.

Another strange partnership is between the cassique birds of South America and—imagine—wasps!

Usually the poisonous sting of a wasp will kill a bird and severely injure most creatures that come too close to the wasp nest. No wise snake, wildcat, or monkey will fool around with a wasp nest. Yet the cassique birds build their homes in the same tree with a colony of wasps and seem to live in harmony with them.

The birds benefit because they and their young are protected from enemies who fear the wasps. No one knows just what the wasps get from the partnership or why they don't sting the noisy cassique birds. It could be that the birds' heavy feathers protect them from the deadly stings of their neighbors. Or maybe they have an unwritten agreement with some special benefit for the wasps.

The more we learn about God's "dumb" creatures, the more we realize God has given them special instincts or knowledge. He shows them how to protect themselves and their young, even when it sometimes means forming partnerships with members of other species.

More wonderful still is the fact that this same God gives you knowledge and loves you far more

than the animal world. Yes, He does. He says, "Fear
ye not . . . you are of more value than many spar-
rows" (Matthew 10:31).

God's love is specially shown through His Son,
the Lord Jesus Christ. Those who receive Him as
their personal Saviour and let Him reign as King of
their lives may have a wonderful friendship with
God.

Let's thank God for His love and care for animals. But most of all, let's thank Him for His love
and care for us.

The Old Turkey Game

A TRUE STORY
by Marie M. Booth

Marie wriggled her bare feet in the early morning dew. "Ah-h-h," she said. "Nothing like it—unless it's the smell of strawberries or new-mown hay."

Out of the kitchen door came Mama with her sunbonnet askew. Mama dashed everywhere. Under those ballooning skirts and flying aprons, she moved on feet that propelled her like wheels. As she rolled past Marie, she thrust a large dishpan into the girl's hands. The pan was for picking lettuce, radishes, and onions from the garden for dinner.

Marie stalled as long as she dared, still drinking in the delicious sunshine. "Oh, well, I might as well get at it!" she said to herself. Trailing her toes through the soft dirt, she dillydallied into the vegetable garden. The dew off the green leaves sprinkled her bare arms. A long moment was wasted as she watched the prisms in the drops flash red and yellow and blue.

Finally Marie sat flat on the damp ground to cut the lettuce leaves. Mama was strict about how they were cut. "Cut the young, tender leaves one at a time and more will grow in their place. That way we'll have lettuce until hot weather," she had said.

"Will you be taking the turkeys again this year?" Mama's voice floated back over her shoulder. Marie knew it was not a choice. She had to do it, or not have school clothes. She also knew what the job meant—stalking the old turkey hens, finding their nests, taking their eggs, and putting them to hatch under a chicken hen.

A turkey hen made a poor mother. What poults* she didn't step on, the mother took along with her when she went looking for food in the wet weeds; then the young got sick and died. Marie knew it was her job to keep the little guys out of the early morning dew.

She sighed as she thought of all the rest of the work, like helping make cottage cheese and cornbread to feed the little critters. But suddenly the memory of the cardinal-red sweater flashed in her mind, and Marie *knew* she wanted that turkey money!

Mama was cutting a great pile of mustard greens when Marie wandered over to tell her that she would like to do the turkeys again. It crossed Marie's mind that *she* would have to wash that mustard too—leaf by leaf—looking for bugs. She couldn't start the turkeys today; washing all that stuff would take all morning.

---

*Young turkeys are often called poults.

Early the next day, Marie took up her watch for the turkey hens. She had learned a lot last year. She knew that a hen, ready to hide out, always got a restless kind of look about her—a frantic, leading-with-her-beak look.

There! Over there—one was taking off. Immediately, Marie slipped upwind and sank into the brush to snake her way along, watching the bird through the gaps in the bushes.

The hen picked her way down a path, her great sprawling claws scattering the pebbles. Marie knew that however awkward those feet might seem, they were superb tools for clearing out a hole in the brush and pressing leaves and twigs inside to make a nest.

Lying flat on her stomach, Marie prepared for a long morning. She brushed a fly away from her nose, and thought how glad she was that it was too early for ticks and chiggers.

The turkey suddenly made her move, following her beak in a determined way. Marie skittered along in the brush, to keep the hen from seeing her. Sometimes those clever creatures could just evaporate.

But this old gal didn't evaporate. She stopped to scratch in the thick leaves. She picked a little, retraced her steps as if she'd changed her mind, then circled out into the meadow to catch bugs. Finally, she explored the fringe of the woods—all up and down the length of the valley road.

How strange she's behaving, Marie thought. Usually, when the hurried, determined look came upon a hen who must lay an egg, she stole away, straight to the nest.

By this time Marie was tired and hungry. Getting up with the turkeys meant grabbing a cold biscuit and a chunk of ham and eating as she watched the flock for signs.

And then suddenly that old turkey shot into the woods so fast anyone might have lost her. Marie moved out of the sassafras cover. She circled high up the slope of the woodlot and crouched behind a brush pile to get a look at the nest. Sure enough, there was the turkey, turning and scratching and digging on the rocks under the brush.

But why on earth does she lay her eggs on the rocks? She's so dumb! Marie thought. She rolled over then and took note of where she was. This was very important. Last year she had lost a nest or two because, upon returning, she could not find the spot.

"Let's see. I'll mark this rock with a flat rock on top. Then I'll make a big cross on that with this red soap rock, and I'll sink a forked stick in the ground with the fork pointing that-a-way."

Peering out of her blind to make sure the hen was still there tending to business, Marie saw to her dismay that the turkey was climbing gingerly out of the hole in the brush as much as to say, "I don't like this place after all."

Turning tail on her choice, she moved nonchalantly away. She hesitated a moment, stretching her long, warty neck in Marie's direction.

Marie, lying in the brush and watching, gritted her teeth. "That old buzzard is looking to see if I'm going to follow her!"

Back down to the road, up into the woods, down the meadow lane to the creek, and back up the

fencerow went that turkey. When she came up into the barnyard, Marie knew for sure she'd been led on a "wild goose chase" by a turkey. That hen had seen her.

She won't get away with that tomorrow! Marie vowed.

With dawn the next morning came the flap of big wings and the thud of one heavy body after another as the turkeys dropped out of their roosting trees. Marie knew they wouldn't leave right away. She had noticed that turkeys forego the morning conversation that chicken hens use. The gobbler struts and drags his wings, swelling all the bulbous red beads around his head, and cracks up the air with a gobble that would wake the dead.

The sting of losing a nest, and possibly more than one egg, had not gone away in the night. Yawning and grumbling, Marie had fixed a bowl of milk, broken cold cornbread into it, and sat on the back porch to eat as she watched for the signal. No time to fix a hot breakfast—pork side with eggs, hot biscuits and coffee, or even oatmeal. *Wouldn't that taste good,* she thought sleepily.

The flock picked and stretched and flapped. One hen after the other melted into fence corners or faded past the corner of the barn, but none had that sudden, quick look.

It was nearly daylight when suddenly a hen lifted her head, gave the staccato pointing as if searching the horizon, and set out. She moved cautiously but intently. Yet instead of taking the road around the woods, this one climbed steadily up the hill.

Marie was glad. Underbrush for cover was more plentiful here. Circling wide to get the oak sprouts between them, Marie stalked the hen. By this time the sun was filtering through the foliage.

If there was any beauty in that bird, gliding in and out of the shade, Marie failed to see it this morning. She knew the crafty critter was using its brilliant pearl-speck markings to fool her into mistaking them for sun dapples. And the occasional bronze in her back could easily be a leftover oak leaf. The straight dark wing and tail feathers would pass for sticks. A turkey had only to stand still to disappear.

Still, this old bird wasn't so stupid—after that silly one yesterday. In fact she was a rather stately lady. Marie could almost believe the vain thing was sporting a necklace of gray-blue pearls around her long skinny neck and a little ruffle of red on top of her beak.

Yes, she was attractive, and she knew what she was doing! No rocks and bushes for her. Emerging from the woods into a flat area, she walked sedately up to a pile of brush. There was no frantic clawing and goings-on; she simply disappeared into the brush pile.

When the stalking was over, Marie draped herself on a log to rest and munch on the biscuit she had brought along in her apron pocket. The sun was high and warm. A red bird flashed a warning that she was in no-trespass land. Just a few more drowsy minutes, and Marie would have been asleep.

The hen reappeared. It didn't matter now that the girl was there—the game was over for the turkey for that day.

After making a three-cornered sack out of her apron, Marie reached in the nest and brought out a warm brown egg, dappled with dark brown flecks. One, two, three, four, five! Five days gone before she had found this nest. It was a wonder the varmints hadn't found it.

With the eggs at home, she now had 13 altogether, she thought happily. Maybe she'd have 19 or 20 turkeys to sell this year. Maybe—just maybe she'd have enough money to buy a cardinal-red sweater! Marie still smarted, remembering last year. Papa had taken her big fat fowls to market and brought the money back to her. There had been enough to buy the red sweater.

That night Marie had hauled out the Montgomery Ward catalog and turned gleefully to the well-worn place where the pretty girl wore the long sweater. It was cardinal-red, with a deep shawl collar, knit-ribbed cuffs, and had set-in pockets. Marie was happily dreaming of how warm she would be and how bright and smart she'd look in the sweater when Mama sat down with her.

"See, Mama? See, that's the sweater! It has—"

"Yes, I see. It is pretty. But, Honey, you need shoes. Don't you think it would be nice to have both a sweater and shoes?"

"How will I do that? I have just about enough money to get the sweater."

"Well, here," and Mama turned the page to another sweater—a cheaper, maroon one with patch pockets and a skimpy collar. It was shorter and the cuffs would not stay snug around her wrists, Marie just knew!

"And see," Mama continued, turning to the shoes, "you could get these neat black shoes and be fixed up for the school year."

The order was made and the money order bought from the postman.

No package ever brought so little pleasure. The sweater was cheap and a dull dark red. The collar did not sweep comfortingly and stylishly around her neck. There was no deep-ribbed extension to the bottom to let the sweater meet flippy pleated skirts at just the right length.

Marie cried inside!

But the next morning she dressed for school. The horses were lined up in front of the house, and her brother was yelling for her to get a move on!

Hurrying out of the door—halfway pleased with

the trim, black shoes, she was settling that sweater on her shoulders, when she saw their schoolmate Josephine Blunt coming.

"Oh, no!" Marie sobbed under her breath. Josephine was riding her big sorrel and looking smug as usual, and sporting that very same cardinal-red sweater!

Remembering, Marie clutched the apron corners as if carrying jewels. She picked her way down the hill path carefully, vowing through clenched teeth, "I will *not* fall down. I will not lose a single egg—a single turkey! I'm gonna have a cardinal-red sweater before I die!"

"IT'S MY NEW SPORTS MODEL."

Give Me Back My Dog

~ A FICTION STORY
by Sara Ann DuBose

Please give me my dog," Amy begged. "You can tell he's mine." Amy Gaven had come to the animal shelter on a visit with her Girl Scout troop. Imagine her shock and delight to find her own missing dog Muffin in one of the cages.

But Amy couldn't seem to make the people running the shelter understand. Now she could feel tears and temper all at once. It was like they were fighting inside her throat.

"No, I'm sorry," the man replied. "It's against the rules. You'll have to come back with your parents and the $5 fee."

"But they're on a trip. My grandparents are staying with me."

"Well, bring them out here tomorrow and we'll see. Run along now. Your group is leaving."

Amy bit her lip. Her eyes stung, but she couldn't let all the other scouts see her cry. Some of them weren't even in her own troop.

"Come on, Amy." Stacy patted her arm. "You can come back in the morning. He'll have to let you have Muffin back. And just think, you can finish all your pet badge requirements with Muffin."

"I guess so," Amy said, sniffing.

"Look, everybody's heading to the cars," Stacy said. "I'll race you."

Amy didn't feel like running. Poor Muffin! With that hateful man there.

"What's the matter, Amy?" It was Ruth.

"I'm OK," Amy said.

"Have you been crying?" Ruth asked.

"Yeah," Amy said.

"Leave her alone," Stacy ordered. "She's had enough trouble. That mean guy in there wouldn't let her have her own dog!"

Amy didn't try to explain to the other girls in her patrol. Stacy would do that. Besides, she was busy thinking about Muffin and all he had meant to their family.

Muffin had been just six weeks old on Amy's eighth birthday. What a present he had been! Dad had brought him in on a Saturday morning. Amy could remember as if it were last week—but it was two years ago. She and Muffin had become best friends.

That little black-and-white, floppy-eared pup followed her everywhere. He had, anyway, until the day, two weeks ago, when he disappeared from the backyard. Amy had given up finding Muffin. Now, there he was at the animal shelter. But that *creature*, that monster of a man, wouldn't let her have him. *I'll get even*, Amy thought.

"Well, here we are, Amy." It was Mrs. Range, the scout leader. Amy hadn't noticed they were in her own driveway.

"Amy, I'm glad you found your dog. Tell your grandfather. He'll see to it you get Muffin back."

"I will, Mrs. Range. Thanks for the ride." Amy waved a quick 'bye and dashed for the back door.

"Amy, am I glad to see you!" her grandmother called. "Your baby brother has been crying all afternoon with an earache. Guess we'll have to take him to the doctor in the morning. Will you see about him while I get dinner?"

"Yes, Gram, but tomorrow we need to go to the animal shelter to get Muffin," Amy said.

"How's that?" asked her grandmother.

"Muffin, Grandma. I found him. When we went to the shelter to earn points for our scout badge, I found Muffin."

"You mean he's at the shelter?" Grandma gasped.

"Yes, and I just have to get him back!" Amy cried. "They wouldn't give him back to me without my parents present and our paying a fee."

"All right, Amy, we'll work out something. Now run and check on Scott. I have to see about these peas."

Who cares about the old peas? Amy thought. *And why did Scott have to get an earache today? Everything is going wrong.*

Amy held Scott and handed him rattles and toys until supper was ready. She didn't bounce him and make funny faces the way she usually did. All she could think of was holding Muffin and feeling him lick her hand.

At supper Amy tried to discuss plans to get to the shelter, but Grandpa and Grandma said they had to wait and see how Scott was doing.

Wait and see. Wait and see. *It's going to be a long night,* Amy huffed as she automatically knelt beside her bed to pray. She didn't really feel like talking to the Lord, except to ask for Muffin. "Please, Lord," she began. "Please let me be able to go out and get him tomorrow. Make Scott better so we can go."

Amy slid into bed and stared at the ceiling. Scott was still crying. *I've never heard him carry on like that,* she thought. *He must feel pretty bad. I guess I've been kind of selfish. I do want him to get well. And what about the man at the animal shelter? I've had some awful thoughts about him.*

"Lord Jesus," Amy prayed again, "I'm sorry for being so selfish and thinking such mean thoughts about the man at the shelter. Please help Scott to feel better and have a better day tomorrow.".

Being a Christian is tough sometimes, she decided, as the clock ticked on. Amy wondered if Saturday morning would ever come.

A phone conversation woke Amy up. "You can?" she heard Grandma say. "Oh, thank you. Amy will be so happy. I'll send her over right after breakfast."

When the receiver clicked into place, Amy called, "Who was it, Grandma?"

"Mrs. Nunn, next door," Grandma said, coming into Amy's room. "She offered to drive you to the animal shelter while we take Scott to Dr. Evans."

"Oh, that's great!" Amy squealed and jumped over the foot of her bed. "I'll go get Scott dressed for you."

In less than an hour, Amy was on her way to the shelter with Mrs. Nunn. When they finally walked into the front office, she felt shaky and nervous. What if they still wouldn't let her have Muffin? A teenage girl was behind the desk.

"Hi," Mrs. Nunn began. "We've come to see about Amy's dog. She saw him here yesterday."

"He's black and white and about this big, with floppy ears," Amy said.

"Oh, I think that one's gone." The girl pushed a pencil behind her ear. "I'll go ask Dad."

No, Amy thought, *Muffin couldn't have been picked by someone else! He has to be here!* Amy's knees were shaking against the counter. She could feel Mrs. Nunn's hand on her shoulder.

"Well, you may be in luck. Dad's bringing one now."

Amy's heart pounded so hard she could feel it through her T-shirt.

"Hi, young lady. I think this is your dog."

Wow! It *was* Muffin. His ears, nose, tail—everything—was wriggling all at once.

"Oh, Muffin, Muffin! Come here. I love you," Amy said.

His wriggling, squirming, and yipping went on and on, but it didn't bother Amy. He could do anything, as long as she had him back.

"That's quite a reunion." Mr. What's-his-name was looking at Mrs. Nunn, and he even smiled. "There's no charge for this one. She's the owner, all right." Now the smile was directed at Amy, so she smiled back.

"Thank you, Mr. Er—"

"Bonnett's the name, and you're welcome. Glad it worked out for you."

"Me too, Mr. Bonnett. Thanks again, Mrs. Nunn," Amy said, looking from the shelter man to her neighbor. "Everybody's been so nice."

"That's because you're such a nice girl," Mrs. Nunn said, as she gave Amy a hug.

"Not really," Amy said, smiling. "God just answered my prayers through some special people. Can we go home now? I want to see how Scott is and start work on my pet badge."

Jaws

by Gloria A. Truitt

My mighty jaws are powerful.
  My teeth are sharp and strong!
I swim while searching for my food
  All day and all night long!

If you should dive down in the deep,
  In waters cold and dark,
I hope you won't bump into me,
  For I'm a great white shark!

Meet the Friendly Hermit

~ A NATURE STORY
by Gwen Kearney

Are you looking for the perfect pet? One that most of your friends have never seen—one that is fun to play with? This perfect pet will please your parents because it is clean and quiet and doesn't take up much room. And you won't have to empty your bank to buy one or spend hours taking care of it.

Does all this seem too good to be true? Does it sound like the description of a pet rock? Well, it's not. Many boys and girls have found this unusual pet fun to watch and play with. What is this perfect pet? It's a hermit crab.

Usually found under rocks on warm beaches or skittering in shallow water near the edge of the sea, hermit crabs can now be found in many pet shops far from the sandy shore and blue ocean water.

Hermit crabs are interesting-looking creatures. They vary in size from one-half inch to eighteen inches across and wear empty snail shells or other hollow objects over their soft bodies. When a young crab finds a shell that is just his size, he backs into it and uses his tail and one pair of legs to hold himself snugly inside.

Then off he goes carrying his borrowed home with him until he grows too big for it. When this happens, he comes out of his shell to shed his skin. Then he digs down into the sand and stays quietly buried for about two weeks until he is used to his new skin.

Now Mr. Hermit must search for a larger shell to move into. Sometimes he fights another hermit crab for just the right shell. His front pair of legs have pincers that he uses like pliers in the fight and for finding food. He has two more pairs of legs which he uses for walking, swimming, and climbing.

When a hermit crab wants to hide inside his shell home, he pulls in his walking legs and uses his claw legs for a door. Then he stays very quiet and is quite safe from enemies.

Two pairs of antennae and bulging eyes that look as if they are growing on stems add to the hermit crab's strange appearance.

Hermit is not a very good name for this crab, because a hermit is someone who likes to be alone. But hermit crabs are often found in groups of from 6 to 100 or more along ocean beaches. They make good pets because they are fun to watch and will be friendly if you handle them carefully and treat them well. A hermit crab will crawl playfully across your hands and arms if you don't frighten it. They seldom pinch, but if they do it doesn't hurt.

If you decide to have a hermit crab as a pet, you

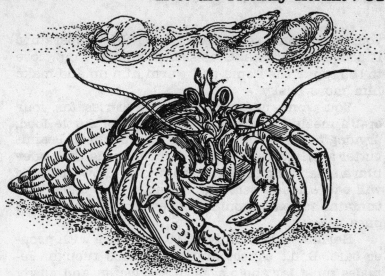

will need something to keep it in. An old aquarium tank or a large fish bowl will do fine. First, clean the container, then cover the bottom with sand or fine gravel. Push a jar lid down into the sand to hold some water and another small lid to hold your pet's food. Or use large, flat clam shells for food and water. If you have other sea shells or coral, scatter them around and the crab's home will look more natural.

Hermits like to try on new shells now and then, so try to have some snail shells that are about his size in his home too. And hermits like to have something they can crawl over and under and hide in. A pile of rocks and a small branch or some coral will make them happy.

If your container doesn't have high sides, be sure the branch or rock pile is not too close to the side, or your crab may climb out and go exploring.

Since crabs like warm places, be sure to keep

your pet's home someplace where the temperature is above 60 degrees. If he seems quiet, a lamp close to the top of his home will warm him up and make him more frisky.

You won't need any fancy groceries for your crab's meals. They aren't fussy eaters. Turtle food, dry dog food, or dry cereal will tempt them. Peanut butter and lettuce are other favorite foods. Just offer him a small amount until you find out how much he will eat. A small serving of special crab chow that contains sea salt should be given to your crab about once a week.

Hermit crabs can live 10 to 15 years with proper care. Don't expect any baby crabs though. Females must lay their eggs in sea water, and newly hatched crabs spend their first few days in the ocean.

A hermit crab makes a good pet for a person living in an apartment or in a home where someone is allergic to furry animals. No matter where you live or what the season, you can bring a little bit of the seashore into your home by having a friendly hermit crab for your pet.

Peanuts

A NATURE STORY
by Betty C. Stevens

Seth Spangler's family had wanted a macaw for several years. One day in 1983, they picked out a macaw at a bird dealer and carried her home in a box with breathing holes. Then they took their truck and bought a large cage for Peanuts, as they named the young blue and gold macaw (large parrot). They needed a truck because the cage was two feet wide, three and a half feet long, and six feet high.

Peanuts was afraid of the family at first. But as the Spanglers learned to move slowly and talk quietly around her, she became less fearful.

One day she had the courage to step on the end of a stick and let Seth's dad carry her around. Soon she was willing to step on the back of Seth's hand.

When her cage door was opened, Peanuts was delighted. With beak and claws, she worked herself around and out the door, then climbed to the perch on top.

Like other young macaws raised for pets,

Peanuts had one wing clipped so she couldn't fly. It didn't spoil her beauty but kept her from harming herself as she learned where things were in the house. The feathers would grow out, should the Spanglers want her to fly around later.

Peanuts can still get anywhere she wants to with her beak and claws. She can go up and down the outside of her cage. She likes to walk around on the floor too, with her long tail trailing behind.

Soon after she arrived, she let Kadoka, the family Siberian husky, know she would be boss. The big dog keeps her distance. She respects Peanut's beak.

When no one is looking, Peanuts will climb up a chair leg and onto a table. She'll pick up any item she sees—fork, spoon, toy—and drop it to the floor. If something is too big to pick up, she will push it over the edge!

If Peanuts wants exercise, she climbs to the top of her cage, gets a firm hold on the perch, and sways back and forth sideways. Gradually, she works up to flapping her wings, showing all her pretty colors and wide wingspread.

The top and back of her head are olive green. The green blends into brilliant blue on her back and wings. Her breast, the underside of her wings, and her leg feathers are gold. Even a single feather is beautiful. The top of each feather is silky blue and the underside is soft gold.

Actually, the macaw is one of the largest, prettiest parrots and comes from either South or Central America.

It is wonderful to think how God has made each creature so special. Besides special fur or feathers,

He gives each a natural instinct to know how and what to eat. Jesus says, "Behold the fowls of the air; for they sow not, neither do they reap, nor gather into barns. Yet your Heavenly Father feeds them" (Matthew 6:26).

Peanuts loves peanuts! She will gently take a peanut from Seth's hand with her beak. Using one claw like a hand, she holds the peanut while she bites off half of it.

With her beak and tongue, she cracks the shell and drops it. She eats the nut after removing and dropping its thin red skin. She eats the other half the same way.

Peanuts likes to ride on Seth's hand and often climbs up to his shoulder. She takes delight in pulling his hair or nuzzling his neck, which he says tickles.

Being outdoors in the summertime is a treat for a macaw. Seth's dad hung a swing perch from the ceiling at the edge of the porch. Peanuts loves to sun her back, then turn and sun her front.

One day Seth's mother took Peanuts on a portable perch to his school class. She put the perch in the car so it rested on the tops of the front and backseats. Peanuts sat on the perch and looked out of the window all the way to school.

She was a good bird that day. She stepped onto Seth's hand and let him carry her around the room. She walked on the floor, climbed the perch, then showed the children how she ate a peanut. Seth's classmates were delighted.

Seth and his family took Peanuts to a veterinarian one evening. The vet said she needed her beak clipped. If it got too long, she would have trouble eating. He held her in his arm, gold-tummy-side-up, and clipped it for her.

He also said she needed more vegetables and suggested some people food. Wild macaws' natural foods are nuts, seeds, greens, and fruits. Pet birds must have similar foods in order to stay healthy.

So now on Saturdays Peanuts joins the family at the lunch table. She perches on the back of an old chair they push up to the table for her. They put down a plastic mat and plate for her too.

The family joins hands while Seth's dad thanks God for the food before they eat. But Peanuts is always impatient. They are still trying to train her to wait for the blessing.

They put little tidbits on her plate—bits of fresh green bean, broccoli, lettuce, or spinach, and apple or orange. Usually, after she has had enough, she climbs on Seth's dad's shoulder. If he isn't watching, she will snatch a bite of cookie or cake as he puts it to his mouth.

Yes, sometimes Peanuts is a scamp, but she is also one lovable bird friend—and one of God's beautiful creatures.

Brandy

~ A TRUE STORY
Told by Jonathan Lescheid
written by Helen Grace Lescheid

Brandy, my beautiful golden retriever, was about three years old when I got him on my eleventh birthday. We liked each other right away.

I decided to teach him the boundaries of our one-acre yard first of all. Then I taught him to speak, shake a paw, roll over, and fetch a ball. He was smart and learned fast.

He also liked to tease. He'd snatch my shoe and dart across the yard. The more I chased him, the more he ran. When I stopped, he would return with the shoe dangling from his mouth. Just as I'd reach for it, he'd take off again, his big brown eyes daring me to "get it if you can!"

When school started, Brandy would meet my bus and together we'd run to fetch the cow from the pasture. And what fun we had later, playing in piles of golden leaves! Mom said she'd never seen a boy have so much fun with his dog.

Then one evening after our Bible reading, Mom

said she had something to tell us. "I had a strange phone call today—from a lawyer," she said.

We stared as she picked nervously at her sweater. "He asked if we'd give Brandy back to his former owner."

Her words were like a slap in my face. "WHAT?" I yelled. "Brandy's *my* dog. You can't give him away!"

Mom hugged me close. "Nobody is giving your dog away," she soothed. "I told the lawyer how fond you were of Brandy and that he was your birthday present."

"What's this all about?" Dad asked.

"The woman who gave us the dog is divorcing her husband. Apparently, Brandy belonged to him. He had found the dog as a stray pup and raised him. He and Brandy went everywhere together—hunting, fishing, riding. The lawyer said the woman had given the dog away to spite her husband."

"How awful!" my sister Cathy cried.

"We can't help that," Dad said.

"Yes, but now that he knows where his dog is, he wants him back," Mom said.

"How did he get our name and address?" Dad asked.

"I don't know how he got our name," Mom answered. "But before I knew what he wanted, I gave him our address."

Dad shook his head. He's often said Mom talks too much.

And suddenly I felt as if somebody had turned the cold shower on. "Dad, what's gonna happen to Brandy?"

"Nothing—if we can help it. That man needs his

wife more than he needs the dog. Let's pray for him."

"And for Brandy," I added.

After that, I locked Brandy into the basement at night.

Two Sundays before Christmas, Brandy did not meet us when we came home from church. I bolted out of the car, calling, "Brandy! Brandy!"

"Probably chasing a rabbit," Dad said. "Come mealtime, he'll be here with his tail a-wagging."

At exactly 5 o'clock, I filled Brandy's bowl with dog food and cracked an egg on it—for a special treat. Always, when I opened the back door at mealtime, Brandy stood there, his ears cocked, his big brown eyes searching my face, and kind of smiling, as if to say, "Well, did you bring it?"

Now I held the dog food out and stared into an empty yard. "Brandy!" I yelled. But he didn't come.

Dad and I walked all over, shining flashlights behind trees and bushes, and calling his name. My parents even let me stay up extra late so I could let Brandy into the basement when he came home. Finally, Mom said, "We'll leave the basement door open for the night. He'll probably be there in the morning."

I tossed and turned, listening to the wind moan in the trees. Once I thought I heard a dog whimper by the window. I jumped up and stumbled to the back door. When I opened it, only snow blew in. The dog's dish stood untouched, frozen egg on top.

The next day I dashed into the house after school. "Have you seen Brandy, Mom?"

"No. I phoned the pound but they haven't seen a dog with his description. I also left a message with the radio station."

"That man *stole* Brandy!" I yelled. "We ought to call the police."

I was still mad when we gathered for Bible reading. "Dad, God didn't protect Brandy. He let that man take him. Why?"

"I don't know, Son. Many times God is merciful and kind to the ungrateful and wicked, and He wants us to be like Him. Jesus says, 'Pray for those who mistreat you.' Let's do that, OK?"

Mom and Dad and my sister Cathy, who's older, prayed for Brandy and the man, but I kept quiet. Why should I pray for a thief? I hoped the police would put him in jail.

Day after day, I came home to the empty yard. I moped and even cried for Brandy.

Christmas morning came. Cathy and I opened our presents, littering the room with colorful paper. Lights twinkled in the tree. Turkey aroma filled the house. But I didn't feel like celebrating. How could I when the rug in front of the fireplace was bare?

Suddenly, the phone rang. Mom said, "Hello!—Who?—Yes, yes, of course—sure, come right on over."

She looked at me kind of strange when she came back from the phone.

When a beat-up green Chevy pulled into our driveway, Mom said, "Put on your coats, everyone. We're going outside."

A gray-haired man looked out the car window. He leaned over and opened a door and a large golden ball of fur bounced out of the car and headed right at me. "Brandy!" I cried, holding out my arms. The next moment we were rolling over and over in the snow—in a fit of pure joy.

When I looked up, the man was standing beside his car. I noticed then that he had a black eye and one arm in a cast. "Sorry to have caused you trouble," he said quietly.

"Come in out of the cold, Mr.—ah," Mom coaxed.

"The name is Lovit, and thank you, I will," he said.

I stared at Mr. Lovit as he sipped coffee and plucked at a cap on his knee. "Brandy and I were in a head-on collision. A drunk plowed right into us. I spent one week in the hospital and Brandy, three days. Brandy's got some cuts on his leg." Mr. Lovit's sad, gray eyes searched my face. "You won't mind putting medicine on them, will you, boy? Here, I've got some biscuits for him and a new collar."

"I'll take good care of him," I said, grinning.

"Why are you bringing the dog back, Mr. Lovit?" Dad asked.

"When I lay in the hospital, I got to thinking. Once when I was 10, I lost a dog. Got run over—on Christmas morning. I cried until I was hoarse. I don't want to ruin the boy's Christmas." Silence hung over him like a halo; then he added, "I'll get myself another pup. Best I start over anyway."

"Thank you for your courage and honesty." Mom's voice wavered. "God bless you for it."

He stood up. "I guess I'd better be going."

"Wait. I have something for you," Mom said. She gave Mr. Lovit a New Testament and told him how he could find peace and forgiveness through Jesus. He took the New Testament but hasn't been back.

Maybe someday we'll learn that he accepted Jesus as his Saviour and that's why the Lord let him kidnap Brandy.

Mr. Lovit's name and a few details have been changed to protect his identity—THE EDITOR.

Forest Carpenter

by Gloria A. Truitt

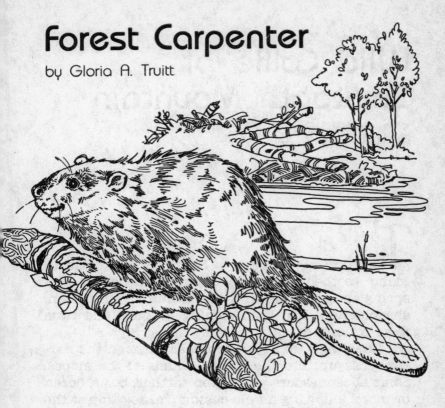

For me, a house of sticks and mud
    Is easy to erect.
I'm also good at building dams.
    I'm quite an architect!

All day long I do my chores.
    I never think of fun,
For I'm a busy beaver, and
    My work is never done!

Wild Collie of Sawtooth Mountain

~ A FICTION STORY
by Bernard Palmer

The camp at the base of Sawtooth Mountain in Idaho seethed with excitement. Because it was spring and the grass in the hills was turning green, sheepherders had been coming by ones and twos from up and down the valley.

They were taking their flocks through the narrow pass up into the grazing lands of the slopes. Some sheepherders went even farther, but a dozen or more, following an old custom, made camp at the foot of old Sawtooth Mountain to enjoy one more evening together before they struck off alone for the summer.

Steve Farwell, son of the owner of the Crescent J, and Bill Watson, one of the top hands on the ranch, came in early with their sheep. They had their tent pitched and supper cooked before most of the others had their flocks bedded down.

Sheepherders were usually older men, wise to the ways of sheep and mountains and used to the long nights alone with their flocks and dogs.

But 13-year-old Steve, dark-haired and freckled, had convinced his dad that he was able to take care of himself. Steve was new to Idaho. He had been born in the wilds of Arizona where a boy learns early to be a man.

"I don't see any reason why you can't take the sheep out this summer if Bill goes along," Mr. Farwell had said. "Bill knows these hills like an Indian, and it'll save me the worry and expense of getting a couple of strangers to herd for us. I think it'll be good for you."

Steve had looked forward all winter to the time when they could take the flocks high up into the mountains to the grazing lands the Crescent J had leased. But now that they were about to leave the last of civilization, he wasn't so sure.

"Are—are you positive we can find our way around up there in the mountains?" he asked Bill, as they walked back to the tent after checking their sheep.

"Sure," Bill said, laughing. "I was almost born and raised on old Sawtooth. We aren't going to get lost."

He was older than Steve by ten years. His lean, youthful face was tanned and weathered from long months in the sun and rain. His sharp blue eyes were alert and quick, missing little that went on around him.

Bill had worked on the Crescent J before Mr. Farwell bought it, first as a chore boy and later as one of the top hands. He knew sheep and cattle and horses. Mr. Farwell had been glad to keep him on.

"Yes, but I've heard of real old-timers getting lost half a mile from home," Steve said.

"We've got a good compass and a map. We aren't going to get lost."

Steve grinned. "I just wanted to make sure. I'd hate to get lost up there."

"Me too," Bill said, stretching out beside the fire and laying his head on his sleeping bag. "There are bears and mountain lions and a little of everything else up in those hills."

Steve shivered at the thought.

"They won't hurt us," Bill added quickly when he saw the look on Steve's face. "Wild animals usually don't want to meet people anymore than we want to meet them. But they will get into the sheep. That's the thing that always worries me when I go out like this."

"Did you hear those men this afternoon, talking about something raiding their flocks?" Steve asked.

Bill shook his head and sat up. "No—what did they say?"

"Myers lost 18, Jimmy Rheim 11, and a fellow from south of Grand Forks lost 23 sheep, all in the last three weeks."

Bill whistled.

"What could be killing them, Bill?" Steve asked.

"It could be any one of several different animals—even a pack of wolves, a mountain lion, or a bear. Most any of those can get started killing sheep just for the fun of it. And when they do, it's just too bad until they are killed. Sometimes a mountain lion or a bear, especially, will do away with 300 or 400 sheep before he's killed."

Steve had overheard those first stories of disappearing sheep a couple of hours before. He and Bill were quiet now as a couple of ranchers walked by their campsite, talking.

"One thing I know," they heard one rancher say to his friend, "it isn't a bear or a mountain lion that's doing the killing over our way. A bear will slash a sheep in the flanks with his claws and so will a mountain lion. But those sheep Myers lost had their throats cut with sharp teeth."

"Like a wolf?"

"Yep, or it could be a dog gone wild. About 10 or 12 years ago there was a German shepherd that turned wild and went up into the hills. That crazy dog got rid of at least 200 sheep before we finally got him. One taste of blood, and he went mad. He killed for the fun of it."

"That happened out our way once," the other said. "There isn't anything meaner or smarter than a dog like that. Believe me, I'm going to keep my rifle handy."

"That's just the way I feel. Why, I wouldn't spend one night out in these mountains without a gun, 'specially now. There's no telling what a real killer might do."

Steve looked over at Bill. That was one thing his mother had remained firm on—no gun larger than a .22. A chill ran down his back. What if he met the killer up on the mountains? What would he do? Both he and Bill were quiet for a while, thinking over what they had heard.

"Isn't it pretty out here tonight?" Bill asked. "Looks like a fellow could reach up and pick a handful of stars."

"It's beautiful, all right." Steve got out his New Testament. Even as he felt it in his hand, he felt safer. It reminded him that God had promised to protect him. He moved a little closer to the fire so he could see to read.

"That's one thing I like about the mountains," Bill went on. "It's so quiet and beautiful. We're away from all the worries and troubles of the world."

Steve opened his Bible to the place where he left off reading the day before.

Bill rolled over on his side and looked at him. "What're you reading?"

"The Bible," Steve answered.

"How come? Did you promise your mom you'd read it every night?" Bill asked.

Steve shook his head. "I read my Bible because I like to."

Bill was silent for a long time. "Aren't you afraid these guys will laugh at you?"

"I don't suppose it'd hurt me much if they did."

Bill leaned over and put another log on the fire. "I don't go for religion much," he said. "There must be some kind of a higher power who made the mountains and trees and stars. But here's the way I've got it figured. A fellow lives the best he knows how. He pays his bills, is honest, treats his neighbors and friends decent, and gives a day's work for a day's pay. I figure if he does these things, he's got as good a chance as the next guy of getting to heaven."

"A lot of people think that way," Steve said quietly. "But the Bible tells us that all men are sinners—" He was cut off short by a sudden commotion among the sheep—a flurry of frightened bleating and barking dogs. "What's that?" he asked, his heart pounding.

"I don't know, but I'm going to find out." Bill was on his feet in an instant.

"Steve! Bill!" someone shouted to them in the darkness. "Something got into your sheep!"

"Come on!" Bill shouted, grabbing the rifle. They started to run toward the place where their sheep were bedded down for the night. Already a small group of ranchers and sheepherders had gathered around. There, at one of the rancher's feet, lay a lamb in a dark, spreading pool of blood. There was an ugly gash at its throat. All the men were talking at once.

One of them reached down and picked up the limp body. "It's not a bear. They don't kill this way."

"It don't exactly look like a lion's work, either."

"A wolf kills like that," someone said.

"Yes, but I don't think a wolf got this lamb. Whatever it was was alone. Wolves work in packs."

"I've known them to work alone."

"A wolf would take sheep out on the range, all right. But I don't think he'd come right in among a bunch of dogs and men to kill."

Suddenly a tawny figure appeared on a rock high above the camp. Steve saw it an instant before the others did, standing silhouetted against the sky. He gasped in amazement. It was not a mountain lion, but the biggest collie dog he had ever seen!

"There's our killer!" several men cried.

The huge collie was poised gracefully on the cliff overlooking the camp. For a brief instant it seemed

to Steve as though the collie wanted to come down to them. His head was cocked to one side, and Steve thought he saw the dog's tail wagging.

"It was a dog all right!" one of the men exclaimed. "I knew that was the work of a dog!"

By that time one of the sheepherders named Myers had thrown his rifle to his shoulder and drawn a bead on him. "This rascal won't kill any more sheep," he said, gritting his teeth.

His bullet hit the rock just below the big collie, then bounded off into the sagebrush with a shrill whine. The sheepherder cursed and pumped another shell into his rifle, but he didn't have time to fire it. The dog whirled and disappeared.

"That's what I said right along. As clever as these killings have been, I knew it had to be a killer dog," Myers insisted.

"Well, what're we waiting for? Let's go after him."

A posse of five men saddled their horses and galloped up the steep, narrow trail out of sight.

"With the head start that rascal has, they won't come within 10 miles of him," an old sheepherder said wisely.

"Wasn't he a pretty dog, though?" Steve said to Bill as the excitement died away.

"No *killer* is pretty!" Bill snapped.

"But I don't see how he could be a killer. He looked so friendly, standing up there on the cliff."

"I've got to admit he didn't look like a killer. He didn't look wild, but you can't always tell. Maybe he's been someone's good dog, but the love of killing got hold of him and drove him out into the mountains.

Whatever it is, there isn't any curing him. The only way to stop him is to shoot him."

"I sure hope they don't catch him," Steve said at last.

It was almost dawn. Steve and Bill were up and packing when the five men came riding back, their faces streaked with dust and their horses lathered.

"I never saw anything run like that fool dog," one of the men muttered. "He seemed to know we were after him. He'd let us catch a glimpse of him just often enough to keep us going. We're going to have our hands full, getting him."

"If we don't, we've only seen the beginning of losing sheep," another searcher put in. "A dog as smart as that one can break us all if we don't put a bullet through him."

Bill thought he and Steve would be going up the mountain alone. But now that the killer dog had been sighted, Myers persuaded him to stay as long as possible with the others who were going up Sawtooth Mountain.

The camp broke up at dawn, and the dogs began to move the sheep slowly up the steep pass in an orderly procession. The sheepherders walked or rode alongside, shouting commands now and then to their dogs, but mostly just keeping pace. The dogs were working smoothly and quietly, pressing the stragglers back into the flock and keeping their own flocks separated from the others.

"I love to watch a good sheep dog work," Steve said as he and Bill Watson rode along together.

"They sure know a lot more about sheep than we do," Bill agreed.

"God must have given them an understanding of sheep that people don't have," Steve said.

"I've never heard it put quite that way before." Bill spoke thoughtfully, then rode along in silence. "Your religion means a lot to you, doesn't it, Steve?" he asked after a while.

"I guess being a Christian is the most important thing in life to me," Steve said thoughtfully.

"What do you mean, 'being a Christian'?" Bill asked.

Steve tried to think of the right words to say. "Being a Christian is having Christ live in you," he said. "The Bible says that everyone has sinned and come short of the glory of God. It also says that the wages of sin is death.

"But God sent Jesus into the world to pay the wages for our sins. He died on the cross for us. So if we confess our sins to Him and put our trust in Him to save us from them, we are Christians."

"I know there's a lot of wickedness in the world," Bill said, "but I wouldn't go so far as to say everybody is a sinner."

"But that's what the Bible says," Steve answered.

"Now take me, for instance," Bill said, grinning. "I don't drink or do drugs or gamble. I pay my debts and all that. You wouldn't say that *I'm* lost, would you?"

Steve was silent a minute. "You're a great guy, Bill. But no matter how good you are—any of us are—we're still sinners. That's what God says, anyway."

Bill frowned and said shortly, "Well, I'll take my chances."

All afternoon the flocks moved slowly but steadily up Sawtooth Mountain, the dogs keeping them together. Finally, the posse volunteered to ride out again to hunt the big collie.

"He's around here all right, young fellow," Myers said to Steve as they rode back to where the herders had bedded down the flocks for the night. "We saw plenty of signs."

"Are you sure he's the killer?" Steve asked.

"Positive. And just as soon as we get something to eat, we're going to go out after him again. He won't get any more of your dad's or anyone else's sheep if I have my way."

Steve and Bill hurried with their work and got it finished in time to ride along with the posse. They rode north along the base of a steep cliff and dropped down toward the place where they had last seen signs of the killer dog. They crossed a small stream, skirted the huge boulders that lined its banks, and headed down again when Bill caught a glimpse of the big collie through the trees.

"There he is!" Bill shouted, pointing toward the spot where he had seen a flash of gold and brown. At the same instant a rifle cracked and they heard a terrorized yelp of pain.

"We got him!" Myers cried. "We got him!"

The men spurred their horses forward, rifles ready to aim. They crashed wildly through the trees, around rocks, and over the stream again, getting closer and closer to the wounded dog. They could hear him running through the brush when they paused to listen, but they couldn't catch sight of him. Bill and Steve rode along with the others until they reached the place where they could ride no longer.

"We're close to that cliff," Colson cried. "He can't get away now!" The men flung themselves from their horses and scrambled up the steep slope.

The dog was ahead of them. Steve could hear him struggling over the rocks and through brush. And in one place where he and Bill stopped to rest a moment, he found traces of blood.

"Maybe he got past us," Steve said to Myers hopefully. He felt sick to his stomach as he thought of the men shooting the beautiful dog.

"Not a chance. We've got him cornered and we're going to finish him off," Myers said.

Finally the posse cornered the big collie, who was cowering behind a clump of brush. He was even prettier than Steve had remembered him. His thick golden coat shimmered in the fading sunlight and the white of his throat was as spotless as snow. Even now, wounded and cornered, he held himself regally, his head high, his front legs slightly spread and his tail arched.

"It's too dangerous to shoot him in such close quarters with these high-powered rifles," Myers said. "We'll have to rope him."

He uncoiled his rope, and they all began to move slowly toward the big dog. The collie moved back, reluctantly, until his back was at the cliff. As the sheepherder started to swing his rope, the dog crouched. Without warning, he sprang toward Myers' shoulder, a deep growl rumbling in his throat.

The man yelled in terror as the weight of the dog's body knocked him down. But the collie seemed interested only in escaping. In two great leaps, he

was gone.

For a moment or two the men all stared into the trees where the dog disappeared. Myers still lay on the ground, fingering his throat and panting heavily. "That crazy dog!" he gasped, getting to his feet. "I thought he was going to kill me! Just wait till I meet that brute again!"

"He's a killer all right," Bill put in. "Now we've got a real job on our hands, tracking him down. He'll be on his guard."

But Steve was secretly delighted that the beautiful collie had gotten away. "The dog sure wasn't afraid," he said aloud.

"No," one of the men said. "He isn't afraid of anything. That's just the trouble. He'll come right up under our noses and steal sheep that a wild animal would be afraid to touch."

"Well, it isn't doing us any good to stand here and talk," Myers put in impatiently. "We may as well go back to camp. We won't see any more of that fellow tonight."

Back at the campsite, the men gathered around a campfire, discussing what to do. Only a sheepman could fully understand the threat of having a sheep killer nearby.

"If we could stay together for a while," Myers said, "we could send another posse out and track that killer down. We've wounded him, so he shouldn't be able to travel very far. But we've got to be on the move. There isn't enough grass here in the lowlands to keep our sheep more than a day or so. We should split up in the morning and let our sheep graze higher on the mountain."

Steve listened while the men talked over Myers' suggestion.

"I know that, but as soon as we do break up, that dog is going to go to work on our flocks," an old-timer put in.

"We should get him while he's still slowed up from the slug he's carrying. If he ever gets well, he'll be four times as hard to stop," Bill said.

"That's right. Maybe a couple of us could turn our sheep over to the rest of you and hunt until we get him," Myers said.

"I've thought of that," the old-timer said. "But I'm afraid this dog is too smart for us. If we try killing him ourselves, he might get completely away from us. Then where would we be?"

"I think the safest thing is to send for Indian George. If anybody can get that killer, *he* can," one of the others suggested.

A little shiver danced up Steve's spine. There wasn't a better hunter in all of Idaho than Indian George Gillis.

Though nobody expected the collie to try raiding the flocks that night, the herders posted guards, making sure someone was with the sheep. In the morning they broke camp and prepared to leave, each to his leased grazing grounds.

"I'm sort of worried about you and Bill being up here alone with that dog on the loose," Myers said to Steve. "There's no telling where he'll strike next or what he'll do. Don't you think I'd better send word down to your dad to have a sheepherder come up and stay—at least until we kill the collie?"

"I think we can manage all right," Bill said,

drawing himself up tall. "Can't we, Steve?"

For one brief moment, Steve wished he were home. But the feeling left, and instead, he felt the thrill of adventure. This was what it meant to be a man—to face danger and accept responsibility. "Yeah, sure," he answered.

"You've got a gun, haven't you?" Myers asked.

"A .22," Bill said.

"That won't be much help against an outlaw dog." Myers turned to leave, then stopped. "Keep that gun handy and don't be afraid to use it. My grounds aren't too far from yours. I'll stop in on you or have some of the other boys see you every once in a while."

"I sure was glad the collie got away," Steve said, when Myers was gone.

"I know you were." Bill swung into the saddle. "But you won't be so glad if he gets into your dad's sheep and kills half of them, now will you?"

"Do you really think *he's* the killer?" Steve asked.

"There's no other answer," Bill said.

"But he didn't look like a killer," Steve insisted. "He looked so sad when we had him cornered, like he couldn't understand why we turned on him. Besides, nobody ever *saw* him killing sheep."

"Well, guilty or not, all the evidence is against him."

"He sure is the prettiest dog I've ever seen. I'd give anything to have a dog like that."

For several hours they rode up into the upper reaches of Sawtooth Mountain. They saw wild game everywhere. Across on another peak, Steve saw a

mountain goat eyeing him curiously and an elk am-
bling through the trees not 200 yards away.

They made camp that night high on the broad
slopes of Sawtooth Mountain. They would keep their
flock here until the grass was eaten short.

"I think we'd better stand watch for a few
nights," Bill said as he and Steve stood together
beside the narrow stream that skirted their camp.
"Is that OK with you, fellow?" he asked, rumpling
Steve's hair.

Steve nodded. It would be hard to stay awake in
the night stillness, but it was their job to protect the
sheep.

They built a small fire out near the sheep and
sat down beside it, shivering in the night air. The
flock was quiet except for an occasional bleat from a
lamb that had lost its mother. The dogs were asleep
nearby, but Steve knew they'd be awake at the least
unusual sound.

"I wonder where that big collie is tonight?"
Steve said after a time.

"I was thinking about him too," Bill admitted.

"He could have been hurt bad from that bullet
wound, couldn't he?" Steve asked.

"I suppose. It could get infected. I guess old
Indian George'll be on his trail in a day or two, and
that'll be the end of that big fellow."

A hoot owl called out, and from across the way a
timber wolf took up the cry. The haunting wail lin-
gered in the night air.

Steve pulled out the small Bible he carried in his
jacket pocket.

"You're a funny guy, Steve," Bill said, after Steve

had read silently for a time.

"How's that?" Steve asked.

"Carrying a Bible with you and reading it and not being ashamed to let a fellow know you're a Christian. Still, you're no sissy."

Steve would have spoken, but the sheep dog at his elbow leaped to her feet and started barking.

"What's that?" Bill asked. He put his hand on the dog's bristling neck, and she quieted a little.

"I don't hear anything," Steve said.

"*I* do," said Bill as he got to his feet and stepped around the tent.

Steve could hear the deep, rumbling growl of the sheep dog at his side as he advanced cautiously, step by step, around the tent. Then he heard another sound off to his right: a soft pleading sound. He turned, and there lay the massive collie, his big brown eyes turned up to Steve. However, the collie's ears went back and the hairs on his neck bristled when Steve approached him.

"Now, fella," Steve said softly, "I'm not going to hurt you." Slowly, he dropped to his knees and put his hand on the big dog's head. For just an instant he felt the animal tremble. But then, sensing Steve's friendliness, the dog relaxed.

Steve stroked the dog's head gently and talked to him. The collie whimpered again, like a baby in pain, and pressed close to his newly found friend. "There, there, fella—we're not going to hurt you."

Bill had come up and knelt beside him, but Steve didn't hear him until he spoke. "That's where the rifle bullet got him," Bill said, tracing his finger lightly across the raw, jagged tear along the collie's

back. "We'll have to take care of that. Come on, old
boy. We're not going to hurt you."

Steve and Bill got to their feet. Together they got
the big dog back to their tent and washed out the
wound with a strong antiseptic. The collie winced
under the sting of it and yelped with pain, but he
didn't bite or claw at them.

"He doesn't act like a killer, I'll say that for
him," Bill said, when they had finished and the dog
was sleeping quietly at their feet.

Steve reached down and stroked the dog's silken
hair. "I know he isn't," he said. "I just *know* it."

The collie opened his eyes and looked around.
"What's your name, boy?" Steve asked.

"I don't think he's going to tell you," Bill said
good-naturedly.

"Well, then I guess I'll name you myself. Blaze is
a good name for you. Come on, Blaze."

The big collie turned and looked at Steve, then
dropped his head to his paws and went back to sleep.
Bill and Steve looked at each other and grinned.

"I wonder what we do now," Bill said. "I sure
can't bring myself to shoot that dog. But the Indian
will get him in a day or two anyway."

Steve felt sick. For a few minutes, he had forgot-
ten that they were out after the dog, or that Indian
George would be roaming the mountain slopes looking for him. And Myers had insisted on looking in on
them from time to time too. If he or one of the others
ever saw the dog, they'd kill him without even trying
to find out for sure if he was the killer.

Then Steve had an idea. They could hide the dog
now since Bill didn't seem to think Blaze was a killer

either.

"Would—would you help me take him up to the cave we saw last night?" he asked Bill.

"Sure. But I think we'd better carry him so the hunter's dogs won't be able to track him there."

"And you won't tell Indian George or Myers or one of the others, will you?" Steve asked anxiously.

"I guess not, if you don't want me to. This dog wouldn't hurt anyone, but Myers hates him."

As soon as it was light, they struggled up the steep slope, carrying the collie to the cave. It was an ideal spot for such a purpose, with a stream not too far away and bushes hiding the entrance. They tied Blaze in the cave with a short piece of rope, then brought him a pail of water and a rabbit Steve had killed the evening before.

"Now just take it easy, old man, and we'll be back to see you tonight."

Steve knelt beside the big dog to pet him once more. And then on impulse, he bowed his head and prayed aloud: "O Heavenly Father, be with Blaze and keep him safe from harm. Please keep him from Indian George and all the men who are trying to kill him. In Jesus' name, Amen."

When Steve got to his feet, he saw that Bill was still standing with his head bowed.

The next afternoon Steve and Bill were both out with the sheep when Myers and another sheepherder came by. "How are things going for you, young fellows?" he asked.

"OK," Bill told him.

"Have you lost any sheep yet?" Myers asked.

Bill shook his head. "Haven't had any kind of

trouble."

"That's good. We haven't caught up with that rascal collie yet, but Indian George will be on the job in the morning. It won't take him long to track him down."

Steve and Bill looked at each other but said nothing.

"Well, we'll be on our way," Myers said.

When they were gone, Steve turned to Bill. "That was close!"

The wound on Blaze's back responded to treatment better than they had thought it would. In a few days it began to heal, and he romped and played with Steve and Bill when they came to feed him.

Blaze soon learned what time of day to expect them and would be standing patiently at the very end of his rope, staring toward the mouth of the cave. And, unlike most dogs, he didn't push and shove to get his meal, but waited until they set the pan down before him and stepped back. Then, and only then, would he eat. He had real manners.

Steve had just come back from feeding the collie one afternoon several days later when Indian George walked into the camp. He had two trail hounds on leashes fastened to his waist, his pack on his back, and his big rifle cradled in his arms. Steve had never seen the Indian hunter before, but he recognized him at once and his heart leaped to his throat.

"You boys been having any trouble?" the Indian asked without taking time to greet them.

Bill shook his head.

"How many sheep have you lost up here?"

"Not a one."

"That killer dog got seven from Myers last night," the Indian said.

Steve looked at Bill quickly. That proved it! Blaze had nothing to do with the killings.

"I told Myers I'd get him in a week." With that the Indian hunter gave a sharp command to his dogs and went off through the woods.

"That settles it," Steve said excitedly as soon as Indian George was out of sight. "Now we know Blaze isn't the killer. Now we can let him out."

"*We* know it," Bill reminded him, "but who else knows it? Myers or Indian George or any of the others would shoot Blaze before they would listen to us."

Steve had an idea. The words tumbled out. "We— we could catch the killer ourselves, maybe."

"Hold on. Not so fast," Bill said, laughing. "How do you figure on doing that?"

"We could tie a lamb out by himself and hide in a tree to wait for the killer. When he comes to kill the lamb, we'll shoot him."

"But all we've got is a .22," Bill said. "Still, that would do it if we shot straight. Maybe that's a good idea."

Steve began to drive a stake in the ground 500 yards away from the flock, while Bill picked out a scrawny lamb and tied it to it. "I hate to do this to you," Bill said as he knotted the rope around the lamb's neck. "But we'll do our best to get the killer before he gets you.

"Now we'll get up in that tree," Bill said, indicating a tall oak not too far away. "We'll be in easy range there. I sure don't want anything to happen to this little lamb. He hasn't done anything."

Steve was silent a moment. "You know," he said at last, "that lamb sort of reminds me of Christ."

Bill frowned. "How do you mean?" he asked.

"Christ was innocent too. But He died for you and me, just like this lamb may have to die for the rest of the flock."

Bill started to speak a time or two, but the words seemed caught in his throat. He and Steve were still standing there when Indian George came up so quietly they didn't know he was around until he spoke. "I trailed the killer dog here," he grunted. "Have you seen him?"

"No," Bill lied quickly. "No, we haven't seen him at all."

George turned to Steve. "I know he was around here. My hounds trailed him here before they lost the scent. Have you seen him?"

Steve gulped hard. He could feel Bill watching him. "Yes, I saw him."

"I knowed it. Had a hunch when I was here before, but I didn't do nothing about it 'cause the hounds hadn't picked up the scent yet." He clucked to his dogs. "Come on and show me where he is. I want to get done and back to Myers' camp tonight."

"You fool! What did you do that for?" Bill hissed as they led the way to the cave. "You've been praying all the time that God would spare Blaze. Now you turn him in yourself when you know Indian George will kill him."

Steve could hardly bear the hurt he felt as he thought of giving up the collie. And now Bill had turned against him. But he couldn't lie.

"Blaze isn't the killer," Steve said anxiously, as they walked toward the cave.

"That's right," Bill put in. "When those last sheep of Myers' were killed, we had Blaze tied up in the cave. It couldn't have been him!"

Indian George kept plodding over the rocks, his trail dogs trotting at his side. "I'm paid to kill collie dog," he said. "And that's what I'm going to do—kill collie dog."

"But the *real* killer will still be loose!" Bill argued.

"Let's get move on," the Indian said. "I ain't got time to waste. It be dark by time I get done here."

The boys could see that Indian George wasn't going to change his mind no matter what they said. At last they reached the cave. Steve slowly parted the brush so the hunter could go inside. He hated the moment when the Indian would see the dog.

"There you are, you killer," the Indian said when he saw Blaze. The collie laid back his ears and growled. "You're a vicious fella, ain't you? Well, a 30.30 slug will make a good dog of you!" He laughed at his joke, and Steve turned away, choking back a sob. Blaze tensed and bared his teeth.

At that moment there was a wild, pitiful bleating outside. It was the saddest sound Steve had ever heard a sheep make. A dog barked, and there was a sudden stir among the sheep.

"Something's in our flock!" Steve shouted, running outside. Indian George and Bill were close behind, scrambling over the rough rocks toward the flock. The cry came again, louder and more terrified.

Something was desperately wrong. They hadn't gone but a little way when Blaze bounded past them, snarling deep in his throat. A short piece of rope still dangled from his neck.

"There he goes!" George cried, throwing his rifle to his shoulder. But before he could shoot, Steve had flung himself in front of the gun. "Get out of the way!" the Indian yelled. But by the time he grabbed Steve and shoved him aside, the dog was out of sight.

"Now I hope you're satisfied!" the old Indian said angrily. "The worst sheep-killing dog in these parts for years and you keep me from shooting him! Just wait till your pa hears! And the rest of the ranchers! How do you think they're going to like it when they find out *you* let the killer get away?"

"But he isn't the killer," Steve said, trembling.

The Indian glared at him and did not answer. The frantic bleating had stopped and for an instant all was quiet. From somewhere up ahead, Bill shouted, "Come on! Come quick!"

Then they heard a low, desperate snarl of rage and an answering growl.

"Wolf!" Indian George exclaimed.

When they had climbed to where Bill was standing, they could see them in the middle of the little clearing—Blaze and a huge gray wolf—close to the stake where the lamb had been tied. The collie was circling slowly, warily, looking for an opening. The snarling wolf was moving too, his eyes never leaving Blaze.

Steve scarcely dared to breathe. He saw the lamb crumpled in a heap at the foot of the stake, and was sure there was nothing he could do to help it.

Blaze had closed the circle now until his nose was just beyond the reach of the wolf's snapping jaws. Swiftly, silently, he lunged, sinking his teeth into the wolf's soft flank.

With a scream of pain and rage, the wolf fell on his back to pull away. His teeth slashed at the collie's thick throat. Blaze fought desperately. Finally, his great teeth caught the wolf by the front foot, but the gray beast tore away to stand a dozen feet from Blaze, staring at him and panting heavily. In that brief moment, Indian George raised his rifle and shot. The wolf crumpled to the ground.

Blaze walked slowly, stiffly over to the big gray wolf and nosed him a moment. Then he turned, picked up the dead lamb, and brought it over and laid it tenderly at Steve's feet. Steve dropped to his knees and threw his arms around the big dog's neck.

"There's the killer," Indian George said, pointing to the wolf he had shot. "There won't be many sheep lost from now on."

"I just knew it wasn't Blaze," Steve said, still hugging the big collie.

"Say, I know this dog," the Indian said, taking a good look at the collie now. "He fits the description of a dog lost up here a few months ago by a hunter from California. The hunter stayed around for a couple of weeks, looking for the dog. When he had to leave, he offered a big reward. I almost forgot about him."

"And he never was wild, was he?" Steve asked.

"No," Bill said. "I think they started shooting at him right away. That's probably why he got scared and kept trying to get away."

Indian George nodded, then leaned down and patted the collie. "You kept me from making one big mistake," he told Steve.

That night after Indian George had gone, Steve and Bill were sitting in front of their tent with Blaze sprawled on the ground between them. "Isn't he a beauty?" Steve asked. "I'm going to miss him when Indian George contacts his owner. But I won't feel too bad, just knowing he's safe."

"I—I just can't understand you, Steve," Bill said after a while.

"Huh? How come?" Steve asked, looking up at the young man.

"All this Bible reading. Then praying for Blaze. Then not lying to save him, but a couple of minutes later throwing yourself in front of Indian George's gun to keep him from shooting the dog. I just can't understand you, Kid."

Steve grinned up at his friend. "I just had to save Blaze if I could, but I couldn't lie to do it."

"That's what I'm talking about," Bill said.

"Well," Steve began, "I guess you think different and act different when Christ is in your life. Instead of doing everything to please yourself, you try to please Him."

"I could never be a Christian," Bill said slowly. "I could never live up to it."

"That's true," Steve agreed. "I can't either—in my own strength. You'll never know how badly I wanted to lie to save Blaze, but I prayed and God gave me strength to tell the truth."

"You mean you really wanted to lie?" Bill asked.

"Sure," Steve said, nodding. "And if I hadn't been

a Christian, I would have."

"But I'm not good enough to be a Christian," Bill said.

"That doesn't have anything to do with it. The Bible tells us that salvation is a gift of God. We can't earn it by being good or doing good. 'Believe on the Lord Jesus Christ, and you will be saved' is what the Bible says."

"It sounds simple," Bill admitted.

"The simplest thing in the world."

"Would—would you pray with me, Steve?"

As they bowed their heads to pray, Blaze moved closer and laid his head on Steve's knee.

THE ANIMAL TAILS SERIES

These heartwarming stories, poems, and cartoons will help you discover God's care for all His creatures. Be sure to read all the books in the Animal Tails series:

The Hairy Brown Angel and Other Animal Tails

The Peanut Butter Hamster and Other Animal Tails

Skunk for Rent and Other Animal Tails

The Incompetent Cat and Other Animal Tails

The Duck Who Had Goosebumps and Other Animal Tails

The Pint-Sized Piglet and Other Animal Tails